HUNTER'S TRUCE

THE HUNTER

BOOK ONE

ELLE BEAUMONT

Midnight Tide
PUBLISHING

Published by Midnight Tide Publishing.
www.midnighttidepublishing.com

Cover designed by Aster Reilly Designs.
www.asteriellydesigns.com

Edited by
Meg Dailey
thedaileyeditor.wordpress.com/editing-services

Character Art by
Natascia Mora
www.instagram.com/moranatascia

Content Warnings

This content contains depictions of graphic violence, profanity, gore, mention of sexual assault, and mention of abuse.

NATAS
MOF

CONTENTS

Zachary,

My dearest, annoying little brother.

None of this would be possible if it weren't for our late night writing sessions, text-based RPGs, or running amok in the woods with paintballs guns.

ONE

The scent of blood was all around me, metallic and heady. It always made me yearn for a hunt, to sink my canines into the flesh of a deer. But the smell wasn't from a fresh kill I'd managed to take down. Rather, the aroma of butchered meat was from the shop next door.

I sank deeply into my down-feather mattress, forcing my eyes shut as the new day's sun threatened to fully rouse me.

Heavy footsteps in the hall only added to the mounting frustration; then they dared to step into my room, to creep up next to my bed.

"It's time to wake up," Liesel's spirited voice announced.

When I didn't so much as move, she took it as a challenge.

Liesel shook me violently by the shoulders. "Niklaus! Mama says to get your slumbering ass out of bed."

Ass? My brows furrowed in question, and I sat up. "She didn't. That was all you." I groaned, rubbing the sleep from my eyes. Our mother would never use such coarse language, and I would know. I'd struck every nerve possible when I was a pup.

Liesel's yellow eyes sparkled with mischief. "You've caught me."

"I think I should remain in bed. There is little going on today, and I'm sure you all can manage without me."

I rolled over again, but quick fingers trapped the blanket and yanked it off me. My sister was a persistent little demon. Five years younger than me, she was just turning seventeen today and still possessed the rounded cheeks of youth. It lent her a cherubic appearance, with a smattering of freckles over the bridge of her upturned nose.

"You will wake up!" Her fist connected with my shoulder, and I quickly roused from bed, standing to hover over her with a mock glare.

Liesel stumbled backward and landed on her backside with a scowl.

Chuckling, I crossed the room to my dresser and pulled out a pair of trousers and a linen shirt.

Liesel offered a scowl in return, promptly sticking her tongue out at me as she stood again.

The potent aroma of blood clung to her. Crimson specks had long since dried on her tan apron. It was commonplace for all of us to have blood caked beneath our fingertips, smeared on our clothing, and the scent of death clinging to us. For we were the village of Walddorf's only butcher shop, and we also happened to live beside it.

Home to Lubrecht Aldridge, and eventually us too. Liesel had been born here, and it had been my home since I was five. Not that I recall anything prior to my days here.

"Why are you lingering, Li?" I scratch under my chin, rough stubble meeting my fingers.

"I'm hunting today."

When I didn't respond, she shook her head.

"Mama said I could, and that we could go as a pack since it *is* my birthday."

Hunting was essential to us. The need hummed in our veins, and with every full moon, we gave ourselves over to the power above, unable to fight the hold she had on us. But Abendrot had long ago betrayed the very ones who founded the kingdom—the wolves.

"We are safer in numbers," Liesel added.

I wouldn't argue with that, but it wasn't *safe*, and it hadn't been for a hundred years.

"Still," I said, glancing over my shoulder as I walked by her. "Do you think you'll actually catch something this time?" Before she had the chance to lob the nearest object at me, I darted out of my room and down the narrow hallway.

Wide, wooden floorboards creaked with contempt as I traveled over them.

"Niklaus, are you teasing your sister again?" Mama called up the stairwell.

I twisted around to lift my brow at Liesel, who was following behind me. She halted at the top of the stairs, and I reached up to grab at her long, red braid. "Am I?" I muttered, but Liesel didn't answer.

"Well, come down here, Lu needs a hand in the shop. The Seidels just placed a big order and they're waiting on it."

I snorted and jogged down the remainder of the stairs, rounding the corner into the kitchen. My mother had her back to me as she rolled out dough on the counter. Flour dusted her green dress, and she smiled even though she shot me a look of warning.

Liesel was her replica. Round cheeks, yellow eyes, and a constellation of freckles along the bridge of her nose. My mother wasn't tall—she scarcely reached my chest—but she was stronger than she looked.

I'd seen her haul a deer carcass across the forest floor.

"We can leave for our hunt after the order is complete. It wouldn't be the worst thing if we had to wait until the sun sets." She sighed, then picked up her rolled-out dough and laid it over the top of an awaiting pie dish.

And I wished that wasn't true for us, but it was. Wolves were hunted in Abendrot, and Walddorf was heavily populated by humans, which made living here tricky, to say the least. A werewolf seen in broad daylight was just an invitation to be mounted on a wall.

What it came down to was, we were safer in the cover of darkness.

Despite this, my mother never wanted to leave. She always said it was a safe haven. I never understood why she would say that.

It was dangerous.

"All right. I'll see what he needs." Before I walked away, I shot another glance at the pie. My mouth watered, I could almost taste the buttery cinnamon delight.

"Go," my mother laughed and flicked flour at me.

I turned away, chuckling as I ventured to the door and pushed it open. Immediately, the sun shone on my face with the summer's strength. I shielded my eyes and walked toward the butcher shop.

Lu hurled logs into the smoker, and clouds of black puffed up from the chimney. Lubrecht was a gracious man. Although imposing in stature, he was a gentleman through and through. Our situation was complicated, to say the least. My mother and I had run from Hilde, our old town, and searched for solace in Walddorf. He'd welcomed us into his home and allowed a pregnant woman and her son in need to live with him. It was no wonder my mother fell for him so swiftly.

Lu didn't know what we were, and yet he brought us in, gave us a place to rest our heads and food to fill our bellies. When he discovered what we were, he didn't seem alarmed.

He warned us, from the beginning, that pigs sat on

the throne and wouldn't rest until the ruination of wolves came to be.

Lu turned around and smiled as recognition flittered across his face. His deep brown eyes held more warmth than any hearth I'd been near. "Well, look who rolled out of bed."

My lips twitched into a grin. It wasn't late, but anything past dawn was well into the day in Lu's opinion.

"Ma said you needed some help?"

He dragged a cloth from his pocket and wiped his hands clean. "Sure do. I can't afford to fall behind on other things. Since you're handy with a knife, think you can complete the Seidels' order?"

"I'll manage." I'd been carving hams and cutting steaks since I was twelve. By now, I could do it with my eyes closed.

Lu opened the door to the shop and led the way inside. I stepped behind him, into the room. Laid out on the wall-to-wall table, a half-butchered pig glared up at the ceiling. It hadn't been portioned yet, and my fingers itched to grab a clever and do just that.

Once, Lu had asked if I ever felt any remorse for extinguishing an animal's life. He'd told me that it was part of nature, but personally, I'd never flinched as the life fled from an animal's eyes. The truth was, I didn't feel anything at all. Not about taking another's life, not about friendships or lovers.

I was born different, so my mother said, and I knew a part of me was missing.Lu grunted as he strung up some sausage links. "You do more than manage." He jerked his head toward the back door. "I'll be out with the smoker if you need anything."

I nodded, then picked up the cleaver. The knife became an artist's tool, cutting and slicing through meat and bone until all that remained of the pig was its ugly head and hooves. Those wouldn't be discarded; we didn't believe in waste. Some people thoroughly enjoyed pickled pig's feet and headcheese. They weren't on the top of my go-to list, but they weren't bad either.

The bell tinkled, and I turned to see who it was. Ansel Scheuner. "Just a moment." I wrapped twine around a portion of meat before me. "Is your wagon ready?"

Ansel lumbered his way toward me. His hair was salt and pepper, eyes an eerie shade of hazel. He was short, stocky, not quite reaching my shoulders. He also wasn't keen on me and never had been. Not that I really cared.

"Go get Lu," he said.

Shrugging a shoulder, I piled the meat carefully and looked at him squarely. A smile formed on my face. "No," I began. "He's busy, and I'm here to—"

"To what, exactly? I don't trust you." His face pinched in disgust as he gave me a once-over. "I don't like it . . . your mother shouldn't have imposed . . ."

Red spilled into my vision, and my knuckles turned white as I gripped the edge of the counter. In two seconds, I was going to jump it, but I reeled myself in— it would do no good to chase off one of Lu's customers.

Even someone as despicable as Ansel.

The man muttered, "Like some whore," under his breath, and human ears would have missed it, but I wasn't human. Not at all.

With my hands firmly planted on the counter, I hopped over the one thing separating us in one swift motion, then curled my fingers around the collar of his shirt and slammed him against the wall. "You can hate me. You can say whatever you'd like about me. But leave my mother and Lu out of it." I bared my teeth at him, lifting him off the floor just a hair. He didn't know *anything* about us. So he could keep his judgments to himself.

I loosed a breath. No need to tap into the beast that lay beneath my skin. I'd made my point clear.

Realization must have dawned on Ansel that he was spewing insults at me when a cleaver was within my reach because he was leaning away and not rising to the occasion to fight. I would have gladly chosen my fists over a knife any day; it was more gratifying when I felt the snap of bones beneath my knuckles.

"I relent!" Ansel shouted, spittle covering his lips.

With that, I released him and stepped backward. "So, we have an understanding now."

"You are the devil's spawn," he spat out, his eyes flicking toward the knife, it was clear that he was considering pushing me over the edge and he wasn't done yet.

A wolfish grin pulled at my lips as I looked down at him. "Yes, well, the old bastard sends his regards."

I motioned toward the counter where Lu had left his

order. I didn't feel inclined to help him, but I was willing to take his coins and shove them in the drawer. Lifting my brows, I extended my hand, waiting.

Ansel's face looked as if it would burst, it was so red, which pleased me to no end. He dropped the gold into my palm and stormed out of the shop.

"Asshole," I growled, then turned back to the portions of pork I had cut before and packaged them neatly.

No sooner had I finished than the bell rang above the door again. This time, when I glanced up, it was Lukas Seidel.

He brought with him a personal black cloud, with his dark brows and stormy gaze. It honestly looked as though someone had pissed in his boots.

It was something I'd grown accustomed to over several years. Ever since he'd started training me, when he recruited me to the Huntsmen. Most knew it as an elite academy for fighters, but in truth, it was only a front for darker deeds—assassins.

After I'd enlisted in the fighting program, I had only wanted the release that giving in to instinct supplied me with. Every time I fought, the wolf within breathed a new awareness into me, and it was freedom —peace.

By the time a year had passed, I was top of the class, and she approached me with a proposition: join her growing team of assassins.

"That good of a day?" I snort, scooping up a portion of the Seidel order.

"It was until that miserable swine strolled out of the shop."

I laughed until I wheezed. "Ansel? He is . . . a blight on this world. In all ways."

Lukas's gaze grew distant, but he nodded his head. "That he is." He visibly shook off whatever feeling or thought had been running around in his mind, and his eyes focused on me again. "Ready to load up?"

I nodded and let him lead the way outside.

Hooves pounded on the dirt road and carriage wheels squeaked as peddlers moved into their designated spots for the day.

Lukas stopped behind his cart and flipped the blanket off to the side with one hand, while the other arm cradled half of his order. He shoved the goods into the back and signaled for me to do the same.

"That's a lot of pig," I said, dusting my hands off on my pants.

"You know how hungry the trainees get," he supplied.

I did, because I was one of them, and I could easily outeat any of the humans sitting at the dining table. When someone pushed their body to the very limit, it tended to inspire an appetite.

"We like to keep our pupils well-fed." Lukas gave me a pointed look and grabbed the blanket, tucking it over the goods and carefully wrapping the sides down so it wouldn't flip off while moving. Then, Lukas tugged a coin pouch from his hip and tossed it to me. His lips twitched into a barely-there smile. "See you soon?"

"I suppose, if there is something worth my while there." Like a new assignment that I could jump into. "What is the training schedule like this week?" There were specific days designed for the academy members, and those for the assassins. On the days the assassins came together, the academy attendants went home or did as they pleased, but they couldn't return to the Huntsmen. The cover story? There were alternate trainees who needed their focus.

Lukas' lips thinned, and he nodded. "On second thought, wait for Sabrina." His sister and I had a little agreement with one another, and he wasn't keen on it. There was no attachment between Sabrina and me. If she wanted to end our arrangement abruptly, so be it. Still, it must have grated on her brother because he always grew exceptionally moody when mentioning the two of us in the same sentence.

I walked back into the shop, shaking my head. The Seidel twins were around ten years my senior and had never married. Not that I sat with them, sipping tea and inquiring about their personal lives. I'd just never seen either with someone else.

Unless someone wanted to count me with Sabrina.

Lu shuffled inside, hanging more sausage links up from iron hooks. "Are you heading out with your ma and sis now?"

"Niklaus!" Liesel's shrill tone shredded the relative quiet.

Two

Liesel sprinted into the shop, cheeks reddened and eyes bright with excitement. A pixie if I'd ever seen one.

"The pies are cooling," she said breathlessly. "Which means we can go." Liesel placed her hands on her hips and met my gaze squarely, defiantly.

Truly, I wished I could argue with my sister and take her by the shoulders, shake some sense into her. We were *hunted* by humans on a daily basis; it wasn't *safe*. If anything happened to her, or my mother, there wouldn't be enough chains to hold me back.

Turning my back to her, I walked to the wash basin and worked the soap into a thick lather. The suds turned pink from the blood running off my hands. "Does it now?"

From the corner of the shop, I heard Lu chuckle.

"You're a bastard," Liesel muttered, shoulders slumping forward as she visibly deflated.

"That is beside the point," I said, wiping my hands off on the towel, then pivoted to face her. Swiftly, I spun the towel around and lashed out at Liesel, whipping her in the side.

She didn't dart away fast enough, and the tail end caught her in the ribs. "Ow! Just proving my point."

Lu banged a mallet on the wooden counter. "Hey, not in here. Take it outside." His tone was firm but gentle. "And be careful out there. The poachers have been out in full force."

"Fair enough." I tossed the towel back onto the wash-basin table. "Don't overdo it while I'm out. When I get back, I'll help with the heavier orders."

Lu's thick brows furrowed, and his lips pinched together as if he was readying to brush off my help, as he usually did. "All right. Take care of them, Nik."

To that, I nodded. He knew that I always did and always would.

Liesel darted outside and leaned against the trunk of a giant oak tree. Behind it, the Heulend Forest loomed, dark and overgrown with green foliage. Even in the light of day, it was akin to night in the very thick of it.

My sister's eyes weren't on me any longer but on the log house, where our mother would exit at any moment.

Sure enough, the door groaned as she opened it and stepped outside. Her deft fingers secured a piece of cloth around her head, ensuring her short-cropped hair would remain out of her face. Not that it would be there for long.

Mama approached us, a tense smile touching her lips. "Let's see what the forest offers us first. It'd be foolish to run in blindly."

"I'll lead the way," I said and, not waiting for my mother to argue, I stepped around the oak tree and onto the narrow path behind it. Knee-high thorny bushes, wild roses, and sapling pines created such dense cover, it was hard to see where our well-trodden path was.

With every step, I drank in the surrounding air, ensuring there were no lingering poachers in the immediate vicinity.

There was nothing but the twittering birds in the trees, and from the smell of it, a nearby deer.

It didn't mean we could let our guard down, though. A human could lurk in the woods, hidden and masking their scent with a wretched tincture from a bloody *witch*. There was a deep-rooted hatred for witches by the werewolves, and the feeling was mutual. It was said the witches long ago desired to remove the free will from werewolves, to become their masters forevermore. Their magic could ensnare us with invisible collars, turning us into nothing more than guard dogs or puppets. Since then, a grudge had settled into place, and from it, mistrust passed down the generations.

The narrow path eventually opened up into a clearing—small, but enough room for the three of us to fit in without being elbow to elbow.

Ravens perched in the trees, protesting our arrival

with loud squawks; they could sense the beast under our skin and what we were—natural predators—and it incited their need to drive us out.

My mother turned her back to us, tugging the fabric off her head, then removed her clothes. She neatly folded them and placed them beside the tree.

Liesel was next, but rather than let her clothing lay on the ground, she hung the articles on a low branch.

I shed my shirt, then kicked my boots off. They bounced off a tree before flopping to the ground. Then I removed the rest of my clothing.

Liesel and my mother shot me a look over their bare shoulders, half scolding, half annoyed.

"Do you want to startle the entire forest?" Liesel groused.

While the ravens gurgled their croaking sounds at us, the rest of the feathered creatures didn't so much as change their tune, but I understood the point. Anyone could be lurking in the woods. With one last sniff of the air and a scan of the immediate area, I determined it was safe enough to shift.

A hum coursed through the air, tension as thick as a braided cord. Not the kind that set any of us on edge. Rather, it was all of us homing in on our senses, reaching deep within to our inner beast.

When I was young, the first few shifts were pure torture as bones shifted, skin stretched, and I took on the shape of a red wolf. But after the tenth successful transformation, it became painless.

Despite the humans thinking our forms were bound

fully to the moon, we weren't. While every full moon we were forced to shift, we were free to change as we pleased any day or night. The days leading up to the full moon were difficult, as our baser instincts warred for control. While it was the most freeing feeling, it could be an inconvenience when one lived in a kingdom bent on eradicating their kind.

My heart thudded loudly in my ears, and an itching sensation crawled across my skin. Then, in a blur of movement, massive paws took the place of my hands. A furred tail flicked in my periphery, bushy and red.

Two other wolves approached me, the same rusty red that peppered my fur. They were large, but still smaller than me. Still, Liesel and my mother were each easily comparable to a small horse, with fur thicker than that of a woodland wolf, and longer too. There was also an otherness to their eyes, too intelligent to be that of a normal lupine.

I strode forward, bumping my head into Liesel's neck. *"Are you ready to sink your teeth into a deer's hide, Li?"*

Her small red figure practically vibrated with excitement, and she whined impatiently. *"Maybe I'll bite you instead."* She launched at me, paws colliding with my face.

"Are we ready, my lovelies?" Mama padded up to us, the patience in her tone dwindling.

Flicking my gaze to Liesel and then back to my mother, I cocked my head to the side. *"Readier than Liesel."*

Liesel growled low but held her tongue.

I shook out my fur, then padded forward, scanning the area and listening to the chorus of birds again. In the distance, a squirrel screeched their upset, but nothing out of the usual.

Together, we crept forward, and eventually, my mother and Liesel moved out to either side of me, creating a potential trap for our prey.

They disappeared into the foliage, even as big as what they were. Their footfalls blended in with the life of the woods, but I could scent them from where I stood downwind.

When the path widened into a clearing, I stilled and flattened against the ground. A young buck with only two points pawed at the undergrowth and then marked it.

The urge to lunge for the creature was strong, the earthy fragrance making my mouth water, but this hunt was for Liesel, and I was only there as support.

"Nik, you know what to do, and I'll only say this once: Do not take your sister's glory." My mother's voice echoed in my mind, and I knew without a doubt, if I'd been standing next to her, she'd be saying those words with a pointed look.

As if I'd steal Liesel's glory.

Liesel rounded on the deer, but the animal didn't flinch. Its wide eyes remained fixed on the foliage as it nibbled on the leaves. From the brush, I could see Liesel's snout poking out, and I wondered when my sister would make her move.

Every muscle tensed in wait, yearning. Just when I

thought she'd never make her move, Liesel lunged from hiding and toward the buck, leaping at its haunches. White fangs snapped at the flesh, finding purchase on the thick muscle, and the buck swung his head as he kicked out. She lost her grip on him as he launched another kick, his head swinging toward her with antlers primed for attack.

I snarled. The only thing cementing me in my spot was my mother's rumbling from a distance.

Liesel dodged a blow to her side and quickly recovered before she targeted the front right leg, chomping down on the slender limb. She tugged and ripped her mouth away before doing the same to a hind leg. Each time, she injured the buck, and each time, he grew more tired.She wore him down until he was ready to flee. His legs gave out from under him, and Liesel let out a victorious yip before she launched on top of it. Proudly, she feasted on his soft belly.

When my sister had had her fill, she lounged in a clearing, but neither my mother nor I relaxed. We seemed to sense it at the same time, the way death hung in the air, lending the woods an eerie silence. An unnatural quiet.

"Get up, Liesel," I demanded.

"It's a poacher," Mama hissed.

Humans often sought the aid of witches to mask their presence with spells and herbs, which hid the stench of a human but replaced it with another scent: magic. It tickled my nose the same way a smoking fire would, coupled with an acidic burn.

We were wolves, relying on our instincts and ties to the earth itself. There were some things even magic had no hope of removing.

The whistle of a bolt sailing by my head brought clarity to the moment. This wasn't a game, and one of us could very well die.

An arrow landed with a *thadunk* in a nearby tree.

I leaped forward, using my nose to rouse Liesel, and shoved her forward, encouraging her to run.

I heard the intake of breath and the sound of a bow's string creaking as someone nocked an arrow, indicating that whatever magic had cloaked the sound and smell of the poachers was gone.

The murderous song of an arrow zinging through the air rang out again, and this time, it found purchase in my mother's flank. She yelped but didn't cease running.

"Just run, no matter what. Keep running!" she yelled frantically.

If I hadn't been worried about returning them home, I would have turned on the asshole firing at us, hunted him like the prey he was, and torn his throat out.

Liesel and my mother bolted forward through the thick undergrowth of the forest, past where they'd left their clothing, and I knew they'd be home within minutes. All I needed to do was ensure they were safe on our doorstep . . . because if this fool followed them to our home, he wouldn't stop. They never did. And the real hunt would begin as he declared that wolves lived in the butcher shop.

I would not take any chances.

Leaping to the side, I hid in the brush until the man came into view, his ruddy cheeks puffing from exertion. He wore a leather jerkin, and the sleeves of his linen shirt had been torn away. Black streaks of dye ran down his face to his chin, and his mouth smelled of rot even from where I stood.

I stepped out of hiding, growling. Neither my mother nor sister wanted to kill a human, but me? I'd been born for this—trained for it. I wasn't afraid of ripping him limb from limb, nor did I care if I snuffed the light out from his eyes. But my sister wouldn't hurt a fly, let alone someone trying to hurt her.

As for my mother, her primary concern was Liesel, and that was fine with me. I could handle myself, but I knew she would round on the poacher if push came to shove. Despite her being a healer by nature in every sense of the word.

At least they were safe now.

The man nocked another arrow, grinning. "Aren't you a prize? Bet you'll feed me for months with that pelt."

Hunkering low, I sprang forward with my paws extended, and in that moment, I realized he had aimed his arrow directly at my heart.

THREE

The crossbow clicked, but the bolt remained in place, jammed. "Fuck!" he screamed.

I descended on the man, snarling, teeth tearing into his neck as though his skin were only paper. Crimson sprayed from his neck and streamed down my fur.

He would hunt no more, and maybe I should have felt something—anything—about snuffing his life out, but I didn't. His blood dripped from my chin as I stared down at the exposed, shredded tendons.

A hint of justification swirled within me. Murdering someone in Abendrot was illegal, unless they were a wolf. That was where the lines were blurred. Hunting a woodland wolf wasn't against the law, and therefore, someone could accidentally kill a werewolf without repercussions. However, if someone slaughtered another person? It was a punishable offense, and it would cost me my life.

Good thing I didn't intend to get caught.

Growling, I turned away from his corpse. *Mama*. The arrow had struck her side. Had it struck anything vital? With a newfound urgency, I raced back home, ignoring the barbed branches and thorns biting into my face and paws.

When I reached the log home, I could hear Liesel sobbing even before I reached the door. I wasted no time shifting back and stormed inside, not bothering to shut the door behind me.

The scent of blood—my mother's blood—nauseated me. She was on the kitchen table, and Lu pinned her down by the shoulders as Liesel fiddled with the arrow sticking out of her hip.

"Just pull it out, Liesel!" Mama, who hardly ever took a truly stern tone, snarled.

"I'll do it." I pushed forward, frowning as my sister stared up at me with tear-filled eyes. This wasn't right. None of it. "Go wash up, Lili." Jerking my chin toward the stairs, I waited until she disappeared from the room.

"Niklaus, your—" She sucked in a pained breath and pressed her head against the table. "Just be quick about it."

Nodding, I glanced at Lu, who eyed me with concern, then turned his focus on my mother. Gently, I pressed my hand against my mother's bare thigh, curled my fingers around the arrow, and yanked it free.

My mother howled in pain.

Lu handed a cloth over as he whispered to her. I took the cloth and applied pressure. None of this should've happened. We hadn't been doing anything wrong; we hadn't broken a law. But the poacher hadn't either, because the damnable pigs who ruled the country refused to make it *illegal* to hunt our kind.

King Ansgar spoke against it as mildly as one would speak against bad manners. Killing werewolves wasn't just bad form, it was *murder*, and if I had to scale the castle walls myself to make the royals hear us, then I would.

Lu cleared his throat. "Did you hear me?" When it was clear I hadn't, he repeated, "Get cleaned up." His gaze went to the blood covering my body, then back down to my mother, who looked to be sleeping. The pain had no doubt yanked her down into a temporary slumber.

If I could kill the poacher over again, wrap my hands around his neck . . .

With that thought, I ventured upstairs to clean up and get dressed.

When I emerged from my bedroom, Liesel was there, staring at a knot on the wooden floor. Her cheeks were red, stained with tears still.

"She's all right," I said as softly as I could muster and crossed the distance between us.

Liesel met me halfway and pressed her face into my chest. Her shoulders shook as she cried. "She could have died, Nik. She could have died, and then what?"

I frowned and stroked my hand down her back. "The bastard won't hurt anyone else ever again." She twisted in my arms, looking up at me in confusion.

Liesel didn't need to know, and I wouldn't say it. If, for any reason, it came back to haunt me, none of my family needed to know a thing. They'd be safer that way.

Liesel sighed and pulled back.

"She'll be okay. Mama is strong." I tapped her on the nose and withdrew. "Do you want to see her?" It had only been a few moments since she'd run upstairs, but perhaps she needed reassurance . . .

She shook her head and quickly avoided looking downstairs. "No. Not yet. Does that make me a terrible daughter?"

My lips twitched, but I thought better of grinning. This moment was too heavy to tease her, as much as I wanted to, so that she'd smile again. "No. That's what makes you better than me, Li." I placed my hands on her shoulders when she refused to look at me, then brushed my knuckles under her chin. "Better than I'll ever be. Take some time to breathe. Mama will understand, I promise."

"Thank you, Niki." She swallowed roughly and backed away, heading toward her room again.

A change had to come to this kingdom. And soon.

EVEN DISTRACTING myself with every chore I could think of wasn't enough to pull my thoughts from what had happened in the woods. All it would have taken was an inch more to the left, and my mother would be dead.

My skin still vibrated with the need to act.

I poked my head into my mother's room and spotted Liesel sitting next to her. Mama had her head propped up against Li's lap, and she seemed to be asleep. She needed it. Mama had awoken a few times, but the searing pain had been too much for her.

Lu had given her a drought to ease the pain but also induce slumber. She'd heal and be well again, but it would take time.

"I'll be back, Liesel," I said softly, turning away.

"Wait, where are you going?" she hurriedly asked.

"I don't know. I need to clear my head." That was the truth. I didn't know where my feet would take me. I was in want of nothing. Nothing but change.

She said no more, and I walked away.

Outside, the scent of the butcher shop lingered. Smoke and blood blended together. It was the smell of comfort—home.

The sun's rays weren't strong enough to penetrate the thick canopy of trees above, which was just as well for me because the heat would be unbearable. Just the same, the villagers of Walddorf milled around, peddling the last of their wares for the day or already closing up for the evening.

I sighed as I walked down the row of carts, eyeing the goods on display. Thick, woolen skins draped over the side of a big wagon, and beside it, leather shoes, shining from a fresh coat of oil.

Hopeful eyes darted my way, imploring me to purchase something—anything—from them. Walddorf wasn't as bad off as the surrounding smaller villages, but it wasn't rolling in the coin either. Every missed sale could mean a smaller or non-existent meal.

"Well, look who it is," came a low, gravelly voice. In my lifetime, I'd not heard it often, but I knew instantly who it was.

My sire. Gregor von Brandt. King Ansgar's pet. But never my father.

It took everything within me not to lash out. Slowly, I turned on my heel to face the male before me. We stood at the same height, but where I had muscle, he was soft. Gregor wasn't overweight, but he wasn't fit either. His hair was a darker shade of red, and his freckles were not as pronounced as mine

Gregor's nose was crooked after years of battles and, likely, fist fights. A wicked laugh reflected in his eyes, which were the same gold as mine.

"You don't belong here, Gregor."

He sniffed. "*Sir* Gregor." Then he stepped forward, his shoulders straightened to puff himself up.

I crossed my arms, refusing to move from where I stood. "That title means nothing when you're no more than the king's lapdog."

Gregor lifted his hand as if he were about to strike me but thought better of it. Be it because of the crowd or otherwise, I didn't know. "Your mother . . ." His voice was strained, and his eyes darted toward the tree line in the distance. "Is . . . she okay?" Gregor scratched at his neck, as if his mating mark burned him.

I hope it seared his skin clean off.

"She is fine." *Fine enough.*

Years ago, my mother had run from the capital city, with me in her arms and Liesel in her belly. My memories of him were scattered, but I recalled one time in particular when he had pinned my mother to the ground, and her screams had filled my ears.

She'd told me to run, to cover my ears, and even though I had listened, nothing could blot out the sounds.

Gregor was unpredictable with his moods, my mother would say. He was inherently dangerous and thought of her—and his children—as nothing more than property. While he was my mother's true mate, Gregor didn't deserve her. And if he thought to disrupt the union between her and Lu . . .

"She belongs to me," Gregor snarled. "Not that bloated human."

I gritted my teeth and stepped forward, slamming my palms against his armored chest. "She belongs to no one, and you better remember that, *sir.*" I spat at his feet. "And I promise you that if you step near her, I'll put an end to your miserable existence."

Gregor lifted his brows and smiled. "Is that so? I've let her play house for long enough. I'm coming for her soon." He sobered a touch; the smirk he wore slid away, and a haunted expression shuttered his eyes. "She is mine." He shoved my hands away before strolling off.

If that was the case, I'd be waiting for him.

And it would be the last thing he did.

Four

A week had passed since the attack on us in the woods. My mother's wound had closed up in a few days, courtesy of our ability to heal faster than humans. Still, we hadn't ventured back out into the forest, and Liesel expressed her growing fears of shifting.

It wasn't right. We should have been able to shift whenever we pleased, to hunt how we were *made* to. But it hadn't been that way since King Vanhal had been betrayed a hundred years ago. He had been overthrown by his councilman and confidante, Lord Tishler. Under Vanhal's rule, we lived freely, coexisting with humans and tolerating witches.

Now, here we were, hiding our true selves in fear of being murdered.

The hinges of the shop door creaked, and I looked up

just in time to see Sabrina step inside. She wore brown skin-tight leather breeches, a matching corset, and a linen shirt. It was uncommon for women to wear breeches—most wore dresses. Her clever blue eyes danced with mischief and a little bit of a challenge, as if she was daring someone to start a quarrel with her.

"Your order is in the back," I drawled.

She slunk around the counter, the heels of her boots enunciating every step she took.

I watched Sabrina's ass sway as she disappeared into the darkened room. Then the telltale sound of fingers sliding over buttons told me she was undoing her breeches. And the simple movements were enough to send the scent of her arousal my way, hardening my length.

There were times I couldn't comprehend what everyone thought or how they felt because emotions, the more complex ones, always seemed out of reach for me. A puzzle I could never solve.

But the baser instincts, like lust, I felt those. Right in my gut, down to the twitching of my cock.

More clothing rustled, then soft *plops* indicated she had shed the last stitch of clothing.

She was nearly ten years older than me, but we were both adults, and one day, when her hand had skimmed mine, I'd not only felt the surge of lust within but scented her arousal and need.

That had been two years ago.

I rounded the corner and peered inside. Despite the

relative darkness of the closet, my heightened vision allowed me to see her bare back. Her skin would've been smooth had it not been for the raised flesh here and there. So many scars. So many stories I hadn't ever heard.

Walking up behind her, I brushed my knuckles over her spine and grinned as she shivered beneath my touch.

I never asked why Sabrina was covered in so many scars because it was none of my business. We all carried our own brandings, some physical and others emotional. If she wanted me to know, she'd have told me.

"Don't turn soft on me now, von Brandt. I didn't come here for tenderness, I came for—"

Sabrina gasped, then moaned as I grabbed her by her braid and yanked her head back toward me. Her bare bottom wiggled into my hips, wanting.

"I know what you came for," I growled, unlacing my trousers with my free hand. The tip of my length brushed along the curve of her ass, and she pressed even more firmly into my hips. "Greedy today, Sabrina."

She laughed throatily and shifted her hand in front of herself. Her head lolled back onto my shoulder as she stroked her fingers over her sex, further perfuming the air with her arousal.

Sabrina sucked in a breath, letting her hips roll with her ministrations.

I wouldn't be so gentle, and she would cry out.

"You didn't come here to play with yourself, did

you?" I spun her around, wrenching her hand away from herself.

She lifted a brow, and her full lips turned down into a mock pout. "What if I did? What if I came to tease you, Niklaus?"

"That's not why you come." I turned away from her and shut the door, locking it from the inside in case anyone should try to enter.

When I faced Sabrina again, she closed the distance between us, peeling my shirt off. She didn't brush her lips against my skin. Instead, she bit and ran her nails along my back hard enough that I hissed.

I kicked my boots off, then shoved my trousers down. Wasting no time, I hauled Sabrina against my chest and ran my hands down her slender thighs before hoisting her onto my hips.

She leaned back, putting her full breasts on display. I bent forward, capturing a bud between my teeth before scissoring it lightly. Sabrina writhed against me, rubbing her sex against my tip.

I walked us to the wall, and she pressed her back against it, then placed her hands on my shoulders. Reaching beneath her, I adjusted myself and she bore down on me, rendering both of us breathless for a moment.

Enveloped in slick heat, I groaned and let her adjust.

Sabrina grabbed my chin and pressed her lips to mine in a searing kiss. Her tongue dipped into my mouth at the same time I started thrusting. She felt so damn good, her inner sex clenching around me every time we collided.

"Faster," she panted, driving herself down harder, and I obliged by quickening the pace. She keened in pleasure, quietly at first, then it grew louder.

"Not so loud," I growled between breaths, and when she didn't cease, I captured her mouth, swallowing her moans.

They drove me on, faster and faster, until my body pounded against hers with a sting. All of my senses were focused on the approaching moment.

Sabrina rose and fell even faster. Then, as she cried out, she clenched around me. Every muscle tensed in my body as pleasure unfolded. "Fuck," I rasped, barely able to withdraw before spilling onto the floor.

Her head lolled back, and she laughed. Sweat beaded along her brow, and small red curls formed along her sideburns. "*That* is what I came for, von Brandt." She moved forward, nipping at my jaw.

I eased her down, grinning when it took her a moment to steady herself. The effects of her release still clung to her, softening her normally sharp gaze. In another setting, I could almost have pictured her curling up like a cat sunbathing. Sometimes, I wondered what that felt like, the true release—body and mind. Still, the physical was enough for me.

Sabrina pushed off the wall and collected her clothes. I did the same and tossed a rag over where I'd spilled myself.

"How can you even *see* in here?"

I couldn't very well tell her why. Even if I trusted her on some level, I refused to endanger my mother and sister. As far as their lives went, there wasn't anyone I trusted that much. "I know the entire shop like the back of my hand." When I finished dressing, I walked to the door and unlocked it, easing it open. Enough light crept in that Sabrina could finish fumbling with her clothing.

No mutterings or footsteps sounded outside the storage room, but before I shoved the door open wide, I glanced around. Empty.

Once Sabrina was dressed, she grabbed a portion of her packaged order from the shelf and walked out as if she hadn't been readying to scream my name. It was just as well with me. It kept things less complicated, and navigating *feelings* wasn't my forte.

I chuckled and pulled my boots on before I grabbed the rest of her order, then headed outside.

Sabrina shoved a crate into the corner of her cart and shifted another in front of her. She motioned for me to drop the meat into it, and after I did, she pulled a tarp over the back.

"I need to get back to the academy. Otherwise, Lukas will skin me alive."

I chuckled. "A want for bacon will do that."

"Men have killed for less."

A bellow rang out down the trodden path, coming from where the shops clustered. I shoved away from Sabrina and jogged in that direction. Was it my sire up to some antics? I didn't scent him.

Or was it a thief?

As I approached the small crowd, I couldn't see the origin, but curses filled the air, and so did the scent of freshly spilled blood.

Shoving my way into the throng, I snarled as someone rammed into my side. They shrank back, seeming to think better of snapping at me. When I got to the center, two men rolled on the ground, fists flying.

One male had a wild head of sandy-brown curls, and the other had long stringy hair the color of straw.

I reached down, grabbing the first male by his shirt and hauling him to his feet. His white teeth flashed against his skin, but recognition dawned on him, for he blinked his hazel eyes at me.

He made a fist and rubbed it over his heart.

I knew Raif better than that. He wasn't sorry, or if he was, it was only because he'd been caught.

"Watch out!" Sabrina called from behind me.

Whoever the other male was, he wasn't about to cease fighting. He lunged forward, fist poised to land a blow, but I stepped to the side, pulled him forward by the arm, and clocked him hard on the jaw. At once, he collapsed to the ground, eyes rolling back into his head.

"Enough!" I narrowed my eyes as I looked around at the tense crowd. Some glared, while others shuffled away and muttered beneath their breath. "Go back to your business, whatever it was!" When they reluctantly moved on, I gave Raif a once-over. Blood trickled from his brow, down his cheek, and his linen shirt had been torn open.

A few members of the crowd griped about the loss of a good show, and two men stepped forward to claim their fallen friend. "Idiot," one murmured.

Sabrina glanced between Raif and me. "What a show . . ." She pressed her lips together and narrowed her gaze on me. "I need to get back to Lukas, but in two days, meet me behind Stein's before the sun sets. Try to stay out of trouble until then." She looked at Raif, and her brows pinched together before she turned around and walked away.

"Out in the open?" I rumbled, but she didn't shoot me a playful glance.

Instead, Sabrina paused long enough to glare. "Behind Stein's. Do you understand?"

"Yeah, behind, I get it." Perhaps I'd finally gotten a new assignment, or maybe she just wanted some ale and some—

Raif tapped my arm, then signed, "He saw *me* and threatened to expose me. And hurt Kina."

The slow, deliberate way he signed *me* was everything I needed to know. He'd seen Raif in his other form, which meant he could continue to threaten him.

Raif lifted a dark brow and continued, "I won't let him hurt my sister."

Trouble seemed to follow him wherever he went. Maybe it was because no one understood Raif. He was as tall as me, thicker in body, and most of the time he was gentle, unless someone threatened his family.

Raif had been mute for as long as I'd known him.

And where he was kind, his sister was sharp and venomous.

I pitied anyone who got in her way.

"If anyone dares to come for you, or your sister . . . they'll have to deal with me."

Raif smiled, and his shoulders shook in a silent laugh. "The Big Bad Wolf."

FIVE

The smell of minced meat teased my senses as I drew closer to my house, and when I stepped into view of the log home, a pie was sitting in the window to cool.

Mama's face came into view as she settled another pie on the sill. She smiled as she glanced down at her handiwork, and then her green eyes flicked up, locking onto mine.

"I find it amusing that whenever there is a freshly cooled pie, you turn up." She waved me inside and turned away from the window.

Chuckling, I strode forward, led by the scent of caramelized apples and cinnamon. If I'd thought outside smelled delicious, inside was enough to make a male's stomach roar in need.

The potent smell of flaky, butter-filled crust drew me to the kitchen. "I daresay it is witchcraft." Walking to the counter, I held my hands out expectantly and grinned as she placed a plate in my hands.

I grabbed the fork and shoved a mouthful of the pie into my mouth. My shoulders sagged as warmth spread through my body.

Liesel padded up to the table a moment later and flopped into a wooden chair. It creaked as she rocked it back.

Mama slid a plate in front of her. "Enjoy. I need to head over to the Ershls. Their daughter is very ill." She looked between me and Liesel. "Try and behave." She shook her head and left us.

Liesel hovered over her pie. "Like we'd tear down the house in her absence?"

"Might do just that." I crammed another mouthful of pie in.

Liesel wrinkled her nose and shrugged. "Did you hear?" When I didn't say anything, she continued. "The king has finally decided on a date for the annual meeting with the public," she said, pausing for dramatic effect. "The end of next week."

I couldn't help but laugh. As far as rulers went, he was oblivious to the real plights of his people. Not that I had personally experienced anything other than that. Although, I heard through the grapevine that Ishkertov wasn't ruled in such a way. However, Ansgar filled the pockets of his council and courtiers, but those who were not nobility suffered the most.

"Do you think this time will be different? That we

could make a difference?" Hope glistened in her eyes, and I didn't have the heart to deny her.

"I don't know," I said because I truly didn't. I could assume the king would laugh and brush off the true issues of the kingdom, but I couldn't say for certain unless someone stepped up and voiced them.

"Then that gives us a chance. We have a sliver of hope that he'll listen. We just need to cry out to him, and then he'll see how much we're suffering."

Her words stirred something in my chest, and I wasn't certain what it was. However, it made me want to try for her, for my mother, and the other wolves in the kingdom.

"So, who is our designated speaker?" I devoured the last piece of pie and set the plate down.

No sooner did I swallow my bite than Liesel beamed at me as she placed her hands on the table and rose with a determined look in her eyes. "You are."

"What!" I half roared and laughed. "Are you joking? I'm the least eloquent speaker and I'd be thrown in a cell for mocking the king."

Liesel's lips turned downward. "You don't have to mock him. Can't you just speak on our behalf?"

Once, before the humans stole the kingdom from King Vanhal, Lord Tishler had been a trusted advisor. It was said that they had formed a pact, that should anything happen to Vanhal, Tishler would assume control of the kingdom. Vanhal had no heirs, and his wife, Queen Matilda, had died from a brief illness.

However, Tishler wasn't as loyal as he pretended to

be. He wanted the throne and the power that came with it. So, he devised a coup d'etat, empowering the humans who were against the werewolves in the kingdom. With the corrupt lord leading the campaign, a rebellion stormed the castle, hunted down the king, and gutted him.

And it was Tishler's kin that sat on the throne to this day.

So why would I hold my tongue when it came to mocking the king? When his line was nothing but thieves.

There were more werewolves in Walddorf than the humans thought. While fear bred their paranoia in regard to wondering which of their neighbors were wolves, the truth was, the humans were outnumbered.

Which meant there were more wolves than I could count that were better qualified than me. But Liesel's eyes didn't waver from mine, and I knew what this meant to her—and, in truth, all of us. I could try; that was all that I could do.

"All right." I sighed. "You have my word. I'll try to appeal to King Ansgar."

IN THE TWO days that had passed, I'd thought over what I could bring up in Ansgar's presence, but all of my options led to degrading him in public. Being thrown in jail wasn't on my list of things to accomplish before dying.

Neither was putting a target on my family.

I'd need to bite my tongue for them and address the problems at hand.

My boots crunched on the gravel as I neared Stein's establishment. The smell of wheat, barley, and hops tickled my nose. Stein's specialized in beer—and it was far more pungent than others. Amidst the sour smell was a sweet one, the fragrant cider that I had no qualms about partaking in.

My mouth watered at the idea.

"I said behind, Niklaus," Sabrina teased from the growing shadows behind the tavern.

I lifted my brow. Sabrina hadn't elaborated as to why she wanted to meet me behind the alehouse, and it had me wondering if there was an assignment nearby. Although, given the glint in her eyes, I couldn't help but wonder if this was more about our physical arrangement.

Dressed in black leather with two hunting knives on each hip, Sabrina looked like a force to be reckoned with, and she was. I had just turned eighteen when I started training at the academy, and I had been at her mercy then. She pushed me to the very limits, until I thought I'd break, only to come out stronger in the end.

She was human, but she was a clever one.

There was a new light in her gaze today, and it told me whatever I knew of Sabrina was what she allowed me to know, but there was a whole other twisted side to her.

"Behind," she repeated and jerked her thumb toward the back of Stein's, then disappeared around the back.

What did it matter if we were beside or behind? The question must have been plastered across my face because she smirked at me as she pulled her auburn hair back from her face.

"There is less traffic behind than in front."

"That clears everything up," I griped and rolled my eyes. "You wanted me to accompany you on a jaunt through the woods?"

"No. It's the on week for the trainees, which means you can't be there." She shrugged. "There have been assignments trickling in, but none that meet your criteria, and I know how selective you've become."

When I'd joined the Huntsmen, I'd taken most of what came my way. Although I never wanted to be involved with children, nor did I want to face down mothers, which really only left me with vile men.

The more vile, the better.

Over time, I'd pruned it down to higher-paying hits because I'd gotten that good, and I damn well could.

I stepped under a tree and reached for a low-hanging limb. Sabrina stared at me, her lips quivering as if she recalled the first time she'd seen what I was capable of.

Seven years ago, she'd seen me haul a man in his twenties into the street. He had been beating Raif, accusing him of stealing his idea for a weapon, when that wasn't the truth at all. Raif was a brilliant blacksmith then and now, and didn't need to steal an idea from anyone.

When I'd finished doling out a punishment befitting of what he'd done to Raif, he was spitting out blood.

She only nodded as she drummed her fingers against her thighs. "Sometimes, I think about that day," she said, confirming my suspicions about where her thoughts were. "You didn't blink, you just . . . did it."

There was no use in commenting on what I already knew, but Sabrina knew how to talk, or at least hold up a one-sided conversation.

"That's when I saw it and knew you could do what I needed from you." She locked eyes with me, blue eyes full of intensity. "I don't regret recruiting you."

Aside from Lukas and Sabrina, there was Raif and his sister Kina among the rankings too. Small in numbers, but mighty as far as skills went.

"We have a new recruit. His name is Breck, and I want you to train him."

My eyebrows shot up. While I was the first recruit they had ever had, the Seidels didn't hand out trust freely. Knowing that Sabrina and Lukas trusted me enough to train a recruit said something about how they felt about me.

"Is he part of the academy?"

Sabrina's lips twitched into a small smile. "Of course. I don't pull people from the streets for this kind of thing." Even though she was smiling, there was a certain level of coolness about her, the detachment from the situation. A lethal killer.

"Is this a paid job?" I muttered.

With the sporadic assignments as of late, the money I'd earned was dwindling. I wasn't hurting yet but would be soon. Normally, the fees for a hit were high enough that I wouldn't feel it. Still, I couldn't simply stroll into the house with new furnishings, exotic foods, and clothing. I had to carefully move articles into the house. A new pan, a quilt that my mother adored, better cleavers and meat hooks for Lu . . .

Something had to come in, and soon.

"Okay, I'll do it," I muttered.

"That was easy," was all she said as she turned around and headed toward a beaten path. "It'll pay well, but not as much as you're used to."

Anything was better than nothing.

There were things I should have occupied my time with according to society. Finding a wife, joining the king's army, or shouldering the burden of the butcher shop. I aided Lu as much as I could, but carving steaks and fulfilling orders wasn't my calling. I'd never been certain as to what truly was—not until I joined the Huntsmen.

She chuckled as he walked down the path. "Follow me."

Leaves crunched beneath my boots as I followed her. A half hour must have passed by the time we came upon the clearing that the Huntsmen headquarters resided in. It was the largest log cabin I'd ever seen in my life, and more akin to what a duke would possess. Three stories high with the second story boasting a wrap-around porch—the windows were strategically placed so that while they offered sunlight, it didn't allow a glimpse into the building so that anyone could spy.

The front yard was much like a courtyard, and stone steps led to the front door, which was just as impressive as the rest of the house. The massive oak door towered over me.

"Still as impressive as the first time, hm?" She grinned and jogged up the stairs to open the door.

"One day, I'd like to live in a place this size," I said, stepping over the threshold. It wasn't just the outside that was impressive. The inside was too: high, open ceilings with exposed beams, prized taxidermy decorated the wall, and as if that wasn't enough, the chandelier that hung from the ceiling consisted of a tangle of massive antlers. That was new.

"Lukas said the chandelier was a bit much, but I think it's a nice touch."

Who was I to critique what went into a house?

"I think we're going to see a boom of recruits. We have a lot of great candidates, Niklaus. You'll be kept busy." She walked down the hall toward a staircase that led up to the second floor.

I followed her up the stairs, and occasionally, the scent of blood and sweat wafted my way. Someone was training still.

Upstairs was grand. The windows offered a bird's-eye view of the forest and into the backyard, which was set up as a training ground. Targets littered the yard, and I had an itch to go outside and try my hand at some of them.

"In here," Sabrina called out.

Following her voice, it led me into the main office. The smell of leather tickled my nose, and I spied her reclining in an oversized chair. She pushed a piece of parchment toward me and nodded her head.

"This is what you need to know about Breck."

I glanced over it quickly. Single male. Twenty-six.

"We deal with a lot of words on paper, but I'd rather meet him. Is he still here?" I quirked a brow and glanced at the door. I assumed the answer was yes because someone was still training in the room below.

It was also the week that the trainees would be sleeping here.

Sabrina pushed her chair back and stood. "Very well. I'll grab him for you. But play nicely. You can wait until you're sparring to face off with him. Understood?"

I sighed. "Crystal."

Sabrina left, and moments later, the sound of boots scuffing against the hardwood floor carried down the hall. But it wasn't her in the doorway.

I assumed it was Breck.

His lip bled from a fresh cut, and a pink welt surrounded his eye. No doubt a bruise would be there within the hour. He was shorter than me, but broader, even more so than Raif.

His eyes were a blue so dark that they nearly looked black.

I sniffed the air. Human. I doubted he would confess

on paper that he was a werewolf. We didn't freely relinquish that information to humans, and while the Seidels were good—as far as I knew—they weren't us.

"Sabrina told me that the Big Bad Wolf wanted to see me." His words held a hint of amusement. "Is that you?"

I stood and crossed the room. "It is, and what are we calling you?"

"Grim works for me."

I nodded. "Well, Grim, you're going to find out how I got that moniker. For now, I want you to rest the remainder of this week. You're going to need it in a few days."

He nodded and walked away, leaving me wondering how the hell I was going to balance the shop, assignments—if I ever got them again—and training the fresh blood.

SIX

Four days of slaughtering pigs. Four days of filling orders. If I hoped to train Breck without hearing Lu complain about my absence, I had to work harder and longer hours.

So, by the time I arrived at the Huntsmen headquarters, the last thing I wanted to do was train someone new. He knew how to fight on some level, but how much did he really know if Sabrina wanted me teaching him?

Breck lounged on the grass, his shirt discarded beside him. He sat up as I drew closer and quirked a brow. "You don't look like you're ready to fight."

Cute words coming from someone who looked like a bruised peach. Beneath his lip was bruised, and the pinkness I'd last seen around his eye had not only darkened but turned purple.

"Try me. I'm always ready for a fight." I stopped a

foot away from him, waiting as he stood. "If you've fought with Lukas before, then you're somewhat prepared for what comes next."

Breck lifted his hands, squaring himself up as he readied for the impending spar. "Somewhat?"

I kept one hand level with my chest, but the other remained relaxed at my side. "I'm not Lukas. There are some things I knew before training here, and others I've picked up along the way." I motioned with my fingers for him to advance.

BUT INSTEAD OF advancing on me, he backed away, inviting me into his circle. Everyone had one—a perimeter in which an attacker could step—and no matter the steps taken, there was always a circle.

Taking the bait, I moved in closer and threw a punch, intending to hit his jaw. However, to confuse his senses, I lifted a knee as though I were going to kick out.

He batted my fist away but didn't see my knee coming, and I was able to connect with his stomach, forcing the air from him.

Breck wheezed, doubling over.

"Don't lose sight of me. You need to be aware of all my moving parts. What good is blocking a punch if my knee can take you out? You're too busy looking at my face when your eyes should be able to flick between my legs, hands, and face." Sweat trickled into my eyes from the midday sun. The last dregs of summer were brutal, and deep in the woods, it was so humid, it felt as though I were breathing through a wet blanket.

"Again," I ordered, and this time, Breck advanced on me. He wasn't as quick as I was, but the power behind his hits was enough to rattle my bones every time he landed one.

I assumed we were at it for an hour, which was enough between teaching and executing what Breck had learned.

My aching ribs said it was time to stop the fighting and move on to something else. So did the bruises forming on my back.

Straightening, I met Breck's gaze, and his eyes locked onto mine. He didn't seem to have any fear, which I knew from experience was both a curse and blessing.

"Let's stop here. Think about what you learned today, but what I want you to do is work on your speed. And how you do that is to weigh yourself down. Wrap grain sacks to your back, fill stockings with sand or grain and wrap them to your forearms and work on throwing those punches."

He looked skeptical but then nodded. "I will."

"Do this every day, unless I say otherwise." I turned on my heel and walked away from the towering cabin. "I'll see you tomorrow."

"Where are you going?" Breck almost sounded confused.

"Doesn't matter." A dip in the nearby pond sounded delightful, but I couldn't spend the entirety of the day at the Huntsmen headquarters. If the coming days required more of me, I had to split my time and be more present at home.

Sighing, I took off through the woods, but this time, my pace was leisurely.

THE PIGS I hadn't slaughtered yet grunted in greeting as I pushed through the tree line. Their mud-bathed noses wriggled as they scented the air.

A boar stared me down, his tusked teeth jutting out as if he could frighten me.

"Your days are numbered," I said with a grin. That particular one hated me, and the feeling was mutual. Every time I stepped into his pen, he tried to attack me, and it wasn't because I treated him poorly. He was just miserable. However, he was nearly of the age and size for butchering.

Entering the house, I frowned, not smelling the tell-tale spices of a minced meat pie. As I turned to glance into the kitchen, there was my mother, sitting at the table crushing what were most likely herbs with her mortar and pestle.

She hadn't returned home last night, as one of the villager's children was sick and in need of her services. Before leaving, she'd let us know she wouldn't be home until late, if not the morning.

Slowly, she glanced up at me and smiled. "Well, look

what the cat dragged in. You look worn out. The Seidels have you working that much?"

"They're adding on to their home and needed a hand with a few things."

"That's kind of you," she said, then patted the seat next to her. "Come sit."

Shuffling into the kitchen, I sat down in the creaky wooden chair. As far as anyone knew, I was just helping the Seidels with their school. Whatever they needed, whether it was helping them build or keeping things in order.

I didn't want to lie to my mother, but what choice did I have? Some would say I didn't have a heart, but telling my mother that I'd signed up to be an assassin would shatter her, and in turn, break me in a way that I wasn't sure I could cope with.

She was good and expected her children to be good.

To be different from their sire.

Despite never wanting to be anything like *him*, I very much was.

Ruthless.

Killer.

Lacking conscience.

I supposed the last was debatable.

Chewing the inside of my cheek, I looked at my mother, truly assessing her. Lines of exhaustion painted the space beneath her eyes dark, and her typically bright eyes were dimmed.

"Why don't you go to sleep? I don't know when you

got back in, but I know you haven't slept in nearly a day."

She continued crushing the leaves in the mortar, adding a new one every so often. "I need to make this tincture for Halterman's daughter. There is a wicked illness spreading in the kingdom. High fevers and congestion, and the villages have little to combat it. Most are waiting it out." She sighed, pausing her ministrations. "Many have begged the king to do something, to offer aid, but they're calling this a plague, and the king has turned his back on all of us." Mother laughed; it sounded bitter to my ears. "Yet he is addressing the city today, as per his annual allowance, and to that I say, good riddance. I don't know that his people will be so happy to hear what he has to say."

That sounded about right. King Ansgar was as useless as the day was long. Any time his kingdom needed him, he hid away, or his efforts were so minimal, they were laughable. Meanwhile, he stuffed his face and pockets with as much as he could.

His daughters, Stasya and Edda, lived lavish lives, no doubt. The finest foods, clothing, and care were at their disposal. Why should Ansgar's daughters have anything less?

I wondered how the man slept at night as countless citizens died. And if he didn't act soon, a revolt was on the way.

"I don't think anyone is pleased when he opens his mouth." I ran my hand through my hair and leaned back, sighing.

My mother reached over and grabbed my hand, squeezing it. "At least in this, we're all the same. Whether you're a human or a wolf, he ignores our plight. The city suffers the same as we do, which is only ensuring the king hides in the castle behind the iron gates." She frowned, shaking her head.

"As a fat pig would."

"Niklaus," she chided, but it hardly had any bite to it. "Be careful with how you speak. He is still our sovereign, and all it would take is the wrong set of ears to hear what you say. You'd be locked away for treason, or worse."

Probably worse.

Sweat trickled down my neck and back, reminding me I still hadn't leaped into the pond not far from the house. It would be a welcome comfort and distraction from the treasonous thoughts rampaging through my head.

Ansgar should be removed from the throne. He should suffer like his people. He should see what conditions he forces his citizens into.

"Anyway. Since you slaughtered the list of pigs for Lu, there isn't anything to be done. He can handle the orders today. Liesel is at Nimblewick's today if you want to stop by. I think she'd appreciate that." Her red braid fell over her shoulder, brushing the table as she returned to grinding the leaves down.

I nodded but didn't say a word as I stood and leaned down to brush a kiss to her head. "I'll see you later on."

She glanced up at me, and her green eyes said what she didn't: *Be good and be safe. I love you.*

I left the coolness of the house only to endure the heat of the woods again. Grumbling, I started my trek to Nimblewick's, which was on the other side of the shopping district and only fifteen minutes by foot.

Despite the threat of a plague looming over the kingdom, Walddorf bustled with life as vendors pushed their wares out in front of their shops and carts lined up with makeshift stalls as merchants traveled through.

The scent of freshly baked bread and rich, burning hearths permeated the air. There was so much life teeming here, and all I yearned for was that damn pond.

"Niki!" Liesel shouted, pulling my attention from the baker's stack of sourdough bread. She held two small pies in her hand and offered one to me. "I was going to eat both for lunch, but I'll share with you."

Beeswax coated her long brown skirt, and she smelled of smoke, honey, and bayberry. Her white apron bore the telltale signs of oil splatterings and had bits of crumbled wax on it as well. She always smelled like the candle shop when she returned home, and it was no wonder why.

I took the pie, sniffing it. Zwiebelkuchen. My mouth watered as the aroma of flaky crust, onions, and bacon tickled my senses. "Not as good as Mama's minced meat, but still bloody delicious." Grinning, I shoved the piece in my mouth, devouring half of it in one bite. One more, and it was gone.

Lifting my shirt, I wiped my mouth off and caught

Liesel staring at my abdomen with a peculiar look on her face which then turned into a frown.

"Where did those come from?" she asked, pointing at my stomach.

I slid a hand to my stomach, roughened fingers dragging over the tender muscle there. "I lift heavy things all day," I supplied with a casual tone, but it didn't seem to ease whatever worry was tumbling around in her head.

"No, Nik," she insisted and walked up to me, pulling my shirt up to reveal the bruises. "These!" Her face crumpled into a mixture of fear and anger, her cheeks flushing with color.

"Li," I began, taking her hands in mine.

"No! I'm worried, Nik. I'm worried about you and what you're up to, but you won't tell me. You don't tell me anything anymore."

The truth was, I did spend a lot of time with the Huntsmen, but I tried my damnedest to balance the time with my family because I knew they needed me to help and protect.

Chewing my bottom lip, I began to nod. She was right, I didn't tell her anything, and it was safer for her that way. Liesel didn't know about my double life, what took me away from her and the shop, what distracted me, what paid a handsome sum and supplied her with the trinkets she enjoyed receiving from me. The new dresses, the latest novels sold in the shop.

Instead of arguing with her, I wrapped my arms around her small frame. "I'm okay, it was just a friendly match. I got sloppy. I promise, that is it. It was someone

I'm training at the academy." At least that was close enough to the truth that it wasn't altogether a lie. Although, I wasn't opposed to altogether lying to my sister if it meant keeping her safe.

I hoped my sister would never change. The world needed more people like her to counteract the ones like me. Gritting my teeth, I squeezed my eyes shut and hugged her a little tighter.

My lips brushed against her temple, and I pulled back to look into her eyes. "I'm going to try to make a difference today, got it?" Tweaking the tip of her nose, I dropped my arms. This hadn't been part of my plan, but didn't we all deserve a better existence?

King Ansgar might regret opening the floor to his citizens because I didn't for one moment believe they would all hold their tongues. *How can I hold my tongue?*

Besides, I had little faith in him, but what could be done other than trying? At least I could be satisfied that I'd spoken my piece to the King of Abendrot.

"Okay." She huffed and scrubbed at her eyes. "I'm going back to Nimblewick's. Please be careful today." She clung to me again, and I gave her one more tight squeeze before sending her off.

After a half hour of searching, I found a merchant departing for Sorensberg City, and they were willing to let me hitch a ride in the back. My companions were clucking hens, bound for none other than the palace itself.

The merchant was a quiet middle-aged fellow who didn't bother me, and that suited me just fine.

Growing up, I never had cause to venture to the city. This was my first time here, and it was overwhelming. The buildings were on top of one another, each attached to its neighboring business, and there seemed to be people everywhere, hiding around each corner, congesting the streets.

Several shops lined up in a row, and some were two stories tall—this was strange to me, for in Walddorf, we had tiny shops or just vendors peddling their wares in the street. Of course, ours *was* a home, so we were fortunate to have two stories.

The people weren't as openly friendly here either. I saw it written on their faces. It was in the way they charged ahead of one another and how there was no polite conversation but there was a scowl at almost every turn.

I hopped out of the wagon as it came to a rolling stop and nodded to the merchant. When I turned around, I saw a towering black iron gate. Behind it, Sorensberg Castle stood, light brown bricks encased in green ivy. The greenery would have helped in blend in against the backdrop of trees had it not been for the dark slate roof. It was the largest building I'd ever seen in my life.

If I'd thought Walddorf was hot, it was even more miserable standing close to so many blasted people.

Their body heat only created a more insufferable environment.

I pushed my way through the crowd. If no one was going to get out of my way, I was going to *make* them. Except a guard halted my momentum by pushing his hand into my chest. I scarcely rocked on my heels as I eyed him.

"No closer, kid."

Flicking my gaze upward, I noticed that the king and his two daughters sat on the first landing. Stasya, the eldest, and Edda, the youngest. It wasn't the unruly, curly-haired Edda that caught my eye, it was her sister. Stasya's hair was as pale as the full moon. She sat composed, hands folded in her lap and her lips pressed together in a thin line. Edda must have said something to her because her shoulders shook, and her face contorted as she withheld a laugh.

The crowd quieted and soon the king began to speak. I found the interaction between the two sisters fascinating. Even as the king spoke, the younger sister tried her best to get her older sister to squirm. Thrice she had to bite her bottom lip to keep from cracking a smile.

Edda reminded me of Liesel. Always trying to make me smile. Always trying to make me better.

My attention slid to one of the city folk, who walked up to the podium and dared to be the first to speak. A woman, no older than my mother judging by the lack of deep wrinkles. "What of the plague rolling through? As we lose our loved ones, no aid is offered!"

"I assure you, we are working to acquire assets to help," Ansgar offered. But it wasn't good enough, because the crowd's volume rose, and they surged forward as one.

The guards were prepared for this and formed a line, pushing the citizens back.

A man took to the podium and gripped onto the edges as if to curb his frustration. "I'm from Bromiel, and though we have much to offer with our fur and lumber, you choose to close us off. We need help."

King Ansgar seemed to consider his words. "We will visit Bromiel soon to see what can be done."

Bromiel needed more than just consideration. That village was poor, and they truly needed aid—quickly.

One by one, citizens spoke their piece, and Ansgar seemed to have an answer for everything. Although they were mostly tiptoeing around the questions.

"I have something to say," I spoke at last, and someone thought they'd cut me off. "No! I have something to say," I ground out, turning to glare at the man. He was shorter than me, and visibly out of shape. His chances didn't fare well. "What of the wolves of the kingdom? Will you offer protection to the beings that founded this country?" My eyes flicked toward Stasya for a moment, and she flinched. "Every day, poachers sweep into the woods and kill werewolves. The sheriffs turn a blind eye, the *crown* turns a blind eye. What of the lives that have been lost, the families that suffer from *murder*?"

Shocked individuals backed away from me, and they

murmured about my audacity, but some echoed my sentiments. For the most part, I found myself in a clearing, alone.

This was personal, but more than that, it affected a grand portion of the kingdom.

An armored male approached the king from behind, hand on the hilt of his sword. I knew his sharp, angular features and yellow eyes a shade darker than mine. My sire.

He shook his head in warning, but I wasn't going to listen.

King Ansgar ran his fingers along his tidy, graying beard. "It is not condoned by the crown to be hunting wolves."

"It isn't illegal, Your Majesty," I said in a clipped tone, curbing a good portion of my attitude. "And with it not being illegal, people will continue to hunt werewolves. It is *murder*."

"And we frown upon murder." He lowered his voice, narrowing his dark eyes on me.

Out of all the things to say, that was how the king chose to address the issue. Ansgar seemed unmoved by the knowledge that wolves were dying by the hands of their neighbors. Nothing would be done. Not if murder was only 'frowned upon.' As though someone had only belched at the table or one of his daughters was being too forward with a male. It was *frowned upon*. What it came down to was that he was more concerned with putting coin in his pocket and food in his family's belly. Not his people. The ones who made it so.

Gregor leaned forward, his dark red brows narrowing, and he shook his head once more and mouthed the words, "Leave it alone."

I spared one more glance at Stasya. Her face was tight, as if she knew the king had just sealed his fate with his lack of inaction. If he would not help the other half of the country, then I would take matters into my own hands.

The king wasn't the only useless one. If his daughters cared anything for the country, they'd speak up, they'd try something, anything to convince the wicked pig wearing the crown to do *anything*.

All I could do was shake my head as the king swiftly moved on to another topic, but it was Stasya's green eyes that focused on me, as if trying to convey a message. I didn't linger to find out what it was because she was already getting a second chance, and no thanks to her blasted father. Before long, I promised myself that I'd come knocking on their door a second time if nothing changed.

Seven

This was Ansgar's first chance, and he had two more to change his ways, to make a difference in Abendrot. Three chances. One for my mother, Liesel and myself. Even though Ansgar didn't deserve it, Stasya did, and so did Liesel. But if the king refused to listen to his daughter, I'd come to his doorstep again, and I wouldn't be simply puffing my chest. Something had to change.

I bit my tongue and walked away from the gathering, but not with my tail between my legs. No, I vowed that I'd have my revenge against the useless king.

Time to make the most of being in the city.

When I emerged from the throng of people, I was at the top of the road that led into the city proper. Unlike Walddorf, the streets were paved with cobblestone, and wherever my eyes traveled, there were people shouting about their wares. By the time I reached the first cluster of stores, I'd already been shoved twice and cursed three times over.

Grinding my teeth, I glanced up at the nearest store and saw a wooden sign with weaponry engraved on it. In the clouded windows, there were axes, arrowheads, and spears. I nodded to myself and strode inside, taking note of the compound bows hung on display and knives on small wooden racks. But it was the hunting arrows that I homed in on.

Hanging on the wall were black arrows with broad silver heads. The tips gleamed in the afternoon sun, catching the light just so. I walked over to them and ran my finger along one sharpened point.

"It'll drop a bull moose with ease," the shop owner offered. "New to the market and not popular yet."

Considering his words, I picked up the arrow and felt the weight in my hand. It was well-balanced; well-made too. "Locally crafted?"

The shop owner grunted. "Yeah, all by the same kid, Raif. I bet he's about your age, lives on the 'skirt of the city."

I couldn't help but lock eyes with the shopkeeper. Raif made this? I'd seen some of his work over the years but didn't realize he'd made it into the city. We were friends, but we didn't always *talk*.

Interesting. "I'll buy one to try out." I reached into my pocket and pulled out a handful of bronze coins.

"You fancy yourself some moose?" the shopkeeper asked and slid the money into a drawer, eyeing me up and nodding. "Huntin' is good for the soul, boy. Enjoy, and let me know how it is."

He had no idea how good hunting truly felt. One whiff of him, and I knew he was only human. I lifted my chin to regard him, then left the shop.

Raif was about to get a visit, and I only hoped Kina wasn't there too.

RAIF LIVED on the outskirts of the city, just inside the Walddorf line. The forest nearly hid his home from view, but the scents of iron and fire hung in the air, telling me I was exactly where I should be.

Metal clanged against metal, and as I pushed through the sapling pines, Raif was bent over, hammering a red-hot piece of steel. His frizzy brown hair was pulled back into a bun, and his muscled arm continued to strike the glowing tip into his desired shape. This sort of work was fascinating to me.

"What are you making?"

He was startled and narrowed his hazel eyes on me before repositioning the bandana around his hair.

Instead of responding, he just stared and squinted his eyes.

"Well, excuse me for not announcing myself." I walked up to him, peering down at the pointed tip, and raised the arrow in my grasp. It could've been the twin.

"An arrow," someone said from behind him. "He's making an arrow." Kina. Hellspawn come to earth. She stared at me with such hatred in her gaze. I never understood it because I'd never treated Raif poorly, and I'd even made it a point to learn to sign. He could hear me perfectly, but speaking was difficult, and that was fine. I was different too.

"Hello, Kina, darling," I purred, slanting her a look that only served to visibly ruffle her feathers further. I turned my attention to Raif and whacked him on the leg with my arrow. "Why didn't you show me these before?" I twirled his work around in my fingers. "I've only seen your old work . . . This is stunning, Raif. Have you shown the Seidels?"

Raif nodded and reluctantly released his hammer and piece of steel so he could sign. "They were the first ones to use them, but they said it set them too far apart from the other work. They want something more mainstream so their work doesn't . . ." His fingers paused, and he glanced at Kina, who was staring at his hands, waiting for him to finish.

I simply nodded, understanding where this was going.

"What are you two up to?" Kina wedged herself between us. She looked so much like her brother. Same dusk-colored skin, hazel eyes, and curly hair. But what separated them was that she was as tenacious as a wolverine, and Raif was more like a bear. If one gave him a wide berth, he was fine, but Kina? All someone had to do was look at her the wrong way.

"Nothing, dar—"

"Don't start with me, Niklaus." She lifted a dark brow.

"Someone is feeling exceptionally friendly today." Luckily, it didn't matter. Sticks and stones, all of that. One thing was for certain: my bark wasn't worse than my bite. My bite was worse. I weighed the arrow in my palm, lips twisting as I considered my next words carefully. "I need a dozen of these. Do you think you can have them to me by the end of the week?"

"That's great, but we need a downpayment from you, *Red*. No payment, no product." Kina waited expectantly.

"How much?" I glanced between the two.

Raif signed his amount, which had Kina making a noise of frustration. "Kina, he is a friend, let it go."

I fetched the coins for him, but he jerked his head toward Kina, who held her hand out. She was beautiful but too prickly, and I supposed too much like myself for anything to ever happen. She hated me, and I simply enjoyed getting a rise out of her.

"And here you are." I stepped closer and dropped the coins into her palm. "Be safe, Kina." I purposely dragged my fingers along hers, and she recoiled before she shoved me away.

Kina growled. "You're infuriating."

"I try to be." I withdrew from them and waved to Raif. "I'll see you soon."

"Tomorrow," Raif signed.

And with that, I left him to his devices and scowling sister.

Luckily, as I emerged from the tree line, a merchant's wagon was passing by. He paused and pointed toward the village proper. "Heading in?"

I nodded and hopped in the back. I could have managed walking, but my muscles still hadn't recovered from the exertion of this morning's exercise, and walking for the better part of the day had taken its toll on me.

This time, I had no companions with me, only barrels of ale.

THE MOON HAD BEGUN her ascent into the night sky by the time I arrived home. Millions of stars peppered the sky, brightening the otherwise dark canvas.

I waved my hand as the merchant carried on, his old mule clopping away. When I glanced at my house, Liesel was opening the door, arms full of laundry.

Her eyes brightened the moment she realized I was back.

If only I'd brought better news to her. It didn't matter if Ansgar outlawed hunting werewolves, there would still be poachers lurking around the corner, waiting to off one of us when we least expected it. But at least there would have been retribution. There would have been some action taken against murdering a wolf in cold blood.

As it stood, there was no recourse for killing a werewolf. Everyone turned a blind eye, and I imagined they secretly rejoiced that another wolf had met their end. In their minds, the world was a little safer for it.

Liesel grinned. "Have fun today?" Her gaze dropped to my hand, and she pointed at the arrow. "Where's the bow?"

"I don't need a new one yet. But this arrow can take down a full-grown bull moose." Lifting my hand, I opened my fist and balanced the arrow there before flicking it so it spun.

Liesel frowned, clearly not pleased with that answer, and she moved to snatch the arrow. "But what happened at the castle today?"

The arrow ceased spinning as I clutched the shaft in my hand and lowered it. "Absolutely nothing. Immovable as always. I don't know, Li. I'll try two more times, and next time, I'll be more prepared." All that we could hope for was for the king to expire and maybe, just maybe Stasya would lead the country as it ought to be. Although I wasn't about to hold my breath.

Liesel chewed on her bottom lip, and when I thought she'd add something to the topic, she didn't. Instead, "Niki, can we go blueberry picking tomorrow?"

My sister never asked for much, and I tried to give her what she wanted. However, I had to train Breck tomorrow, and if Liesel wanted to beat the heat of the day, she'd want to head out early. Dividing my time equally was starting to become difficult. The only saving grace was that I hadn't received an assignment yet.

I could always train Breck in the evening. Tomorrow, Liesel would have my undivided attention. "I think we can arrange for that. But for now, I need food."

"You always need food."

"I have needs, Liesel," I grumbled.

As PROMISED, blueberry picking was earlier in the day. Liesel's bright yellow eyes gleamed in the sun as she joked about having eaten more blueberries than she had picked.

"Quit eating them, Li, we're not going to have any leftovers for that pie you promised." Our mother typically made the pies, but she was busy with the uptick in illnesses, and Liesel had taken over much of the cooking.

She huffed in my direction, and I replied with a puff.

"We will have plenty. It's a full moon tonight, and we'll both be hungry after our change."

That was true. Lu was dreading it, but he knew he couldn't keep us cooped up in the house, where we'd be caged in our rooms and liable to tear them apart only to escape into the night in spite of his efforts.

"That doesn't mean much—I'm always hungry." Shrugging, I took a handful of berries out of her basket and grinned.

"Niklaus!"

I smiled smugly, which didn't last for long because

she had a fistful of blueberries that she slapped—or rather, smooshed—against my face. Sticky, sweet-smelling fragments of the berries dripped from my face and plopped onto the ground. Staring dryly at her, I rubbed my cheek against the arm of my shirt.

"Dirty fighter."

When we finished picking two medium-sized baskets of berries, we maneuvered our way back to the house, and only one of us was still happy enough to bounce their way home.

Lu must have heard Liesel's laugh ring out because he stuck his head out of the shop upon our arrival. "Nik, Sabrina is here. Mind helping her load the wagon? Another customer is lined up."

I nodded and handed Liesel the other basket of berries. "It's all you from here." Moving away from her, I sought out Sabrina, who sat casually on the bed of the wagon.

"Where's my order?" She raked her gaze over me and snickered. I couldn't say I blamed her, with my shirt covered in blueberry guts and my face stained with juice. I must have been a sight to behold.

"Should I snap in hopes magic will spring forth?" I lifted a brow but headed back inside to grab her order. The back-and-forth arrangement we had was compli-cated, but I never knew how to read her moods. Whether she wanted me or simply wanted to give me hell.

When I returned to her wagon, I slid the box into the back and leaned on it. "Happy?"

"Absolutely." She ruffled my hair, giving it a firm yank. "Go clean yourself up," she said with a laugh, then looked up at the fading sun. "See you later?"

Of course she noticed I hadn't been to headquarters today. "Of course. If Breck is able to move today?"

Sabrina laughed. "Come earlier, and I'll make it worth your while."

There it was. A growl rumbled in my chest, involuntary. My inner wolf was ramping up as the day dragged on and night pulled my other form to the surface.

Heading back inside, I did clean up and enjoyed the scent of blueberry pie baking. It took all the strength I had not to devour the entire pie before tonight, and that coupled with the threats gifted by my sister held me at bay—only barely.

By nightfall, the sky burst with life, stars shone brightly in numbers that were too high to count, and the full moon hung against the backdrop. We all felt it, the tug and the itching of our skin as we traipsed into the woods.

This time, we were even more careful because of the attack on the last full moon. Liesel hadn't seemed to have lost the anxiety that came with shifting. The hunter had stolen that from her, and it was unforgivable in my eyes.

"I won't let anything happen to you," I murmured and kissed the top of her head.

"Just keep your senses open and look out for one another," Mother chimed in.

Liesel sighed. "Okay. We can do this," she said, likely more to herself than us.

"We can," I said, and then the sounds of bones crunching filled the air. *Snap, snap, pop!* Shifting—no matter how many times it occurred—broke bones. They shifted, realigned as our and bodies became something other. Luckily, with age, it became less painful.

Our mother went from a small, slender woman to a red wolf. Then, it was our turn as our bodies accepted the moon's power over us.

Liesel shook her head, licking her chops, more than ready to begin a night of hunting.

Shifting was quicker for me than it was for Liesel, the snapping of bones, the way my skin grew fur and bones elongated. Claws jutted out from my fingertips, and in a blink, I stood in my wolf form. Burnt red, not so unlike the color of my hair. Liesel was a smaller twin to me.

Lifting our muzzles to the sky, we scented the air for our meal, too wise to howl even though the urge was there.

"*Quietly,*" Mama warned.

Hunting in a pack was ideal, it was in our nature, but the increase of poachers made it difficult to hunt together. No one wanted to be caught, and the majority would have rather fled than turned on the one hunting them.

But our pack was small. And every full moon, when the moon demanded we give ourselves over to her, we would hunt as a family.

Tonight was no different. And so, we hunted and didn't return home until our beasts and bellies were satisfied.

Eight

Before the sun thought of rising, I rolled out of bed. Downstairs, I found a piece of scrap paper and snagged the inkwell. I scribbled a note for whomever woke first, letting them know I'd be at the academy.

I'd have to train Breck again, but first, I needed to attend to my needs and Sabrina's—as long as that offer was still on the table.

I set off at a jog to headquarters. Amid my trek, I mused over how easy I'd gone on Breck. If Sabrina wanted me to train him, I supposed I needed to go harder. If he was meant to serve in this line of duty, he needed to be pushed.

As I rounded the corner of the building, I caught a familiar scent—Sabrina. I smelled her arousal even from where I stood. When I slunk around the corner, I spied her leaning against the building with her arms crossed.

"Looks like you have me all to yourself, Niki," she purred and sauntered toward the barn in the back.

I watched her walk away, hips swaying, but still, annoyance coursed through me. "Don't call me that," I snapped. "It's Nik or nothing." Niklaus meant I was in trouble, and Niki was a term of endearment my mother or sister used. Sabrina had no place using it.

She turned to look at me, and the expression on her face said she was considering furthering the teasing, but she pointed to the barn. "We only have a limited time."

I followed her into the barn. The horses blinked in confusion, then nickered, wanting their feed or to be turned out. Sabrina grabbed the front of my shirt and hauled me into an empty stall.

It was difficult to explain how I felt after a full moon. My senses were heightened, and there was a silent battle that raged on inside of me as the inner beast yearned to emerge once more. The baser instincts reared their heads, and I wanted to devour food, rut all day, and run.

I peeled my shirt off, and Sabrina discarded all of her clothing until she stood bare before me. Her full breasts begged for me to taste and tease. Dipping my head, I drew one perfect peak into my mouth and scissored my teeth across. She moaned in response, threading her fingers in my hair.

"We don't have time for teasing, Nik."

Grumbling, I pulled my mouth away and shimmied my pants down. "Quick and dirty?"

"You know how I like it," she said, breath hitching as I pinched her other nipple. Before she could chastise me, I hauled her up onto my hips and positioned her above my length, and she bore down on me. She was so slick already that it was easy for her to slide down my shaft.

"Fuck, Sabrina."

She placed her hands on my shoulders, using me to gain leverage so she could rise only to fall back onto me. As she rode my length, I started my rhythm of working with her, pumping into her tightness.

My teeth scraped along her neck, and I sought her lips, only to be denied. Growling, I increased my pace, and she had no choice but to meet my demands.

"Fuck!" she cried out as she collided with me again and again. "Your cock feels so fucking good." Her nails dug into my shoulder, scraping and urging me on. She tilted back, resting against the wall so I could switch my angle up, grinding into her more.

Sabrina's legs tightened around me as she ground herself against me, and I couldn't help but watch. I'd have to remember this as we sparred, how I completely undid her in these moments.

Chuckling, I reached up, pinching her nipple as I thrust within her. I rolled the bud between my fingers until I felt her quivering around me. "Shit," I panted and moved my hands to her bottom as she rode me hard and fast.

"Don't stop," she moaned, closing her eyes as she trembled.

Warmth spread through my body, and my breathing grew ragged. "Sabrina," I panted her name, and as she shuddered around me violently, I held off until it felt as though I'd burst at the seams.

Finally, I withdrew from her, spilling my seed against the wall. I drew in deep breaths, then chuckled as she started to laugh.

"Well, not a bad start to the day," she said, moaning as she shifted against the wall. "Better get dressed so we can head in."

I eased her down, waiting to make sure she could stand before I pulled my pants back up and fetched my shirt. "Suppose we should."

We headed inside just as the new recruits were rousing. Raif must have just arrived, because he stood in the foyer, lifting an eyebrow at me then at Sabrina.

"Why are you here?" I signed to Raif.

"Training a newcomer," he signed back.

Sabrina walked toward the stairs, then paused. "You two can handle the recruits. I need to take care some paperwork."

Raif nodded, and I followed him to the training room.

"You and Sabrina?" he signed.

"Not really anything. Just entertainment."

"I see." He shook his head. "Do you want to sit this out, since you've already warmed up?" He flashed a grin in my direction, and I shoved him.

"Let's get to it."

The Seidels wouldn't be joining us, so Raif and I entered the training room and gave the small group of recruits a once-over. Kranz: he'd enlisted at the same time as Breck. He was taller than me, broad and muscled, and had a sparse scattering of hair on his head. His neck was so thick, it appeared to be an extension of his chest.

Then there was Breck.

And the third and final—I didn't know who he was.

"Who are you?" I cocked my head and assessed him. Whip-cord lean but with a tenacity in his dark eyes that told me to not underestimate him. His rust-brown hair hung to his shoulders, but that would have to be remedied because it'd get in his way.

"Mateo," he offered.

"Tie your hair back. You'll want it out of your face during today's exercises." I crossed my arms and nodded as he complied. "As we progress in our training, some of you may be selected for assignments. Sabrina or Lukas will reach out to you privately to discuss these, and to see if they think you're truly ready. Over the next few weeks, you're going to be tested in various ways. Be prepared.

"Now, since you're warmed up, today's efforts will be spent on scaling the climbing wall as quickly and efficiently as possible." I thumbed toward the far left wall, which was the only one that didn't have weapons covering it.

There was a single rope with widely spaced footholds. In this line of work, climbing walls was a frequent occurrence, and scrambling up and down as fast as possible was important.

"Begin, Kranz," I ordered.

The man lumbered forward and took a running start at the wall, gripping the rope to pull himself up. He got halfway before his foot slid off a hold and his arms grew tired from dangling. Kranz relinquished his hold, and he dropped to the ground, cursing.

Next was Breck. He took his time with the footholds, only using the rope to pull himself to another vantage point. Moments ticked by as he continued to scale the wall, then he made it, ringing the bell at the very top.

"Not too bad, Breck. Now let's see if Mateo can follow that." I turned toward him, lifting a brow in question. "Ready?"

Breck had succeeded because he took it slow, mapped out his course, and he was strong. Mateo could do this if he applied himself.

He drew in a deep breath, then started to climb the wall, careful of where he stepped and what hold he grabbed onto.

When he found himself stuck, unable to move in any direction, he leaped for the rope. There were no footholds to help him; he had to rely on pulling myself up. He hung for a moment, but the longer he did, the more his muscles would scream.

"Keep going. The longer you sit there, the harder it's going to be," I encouraged.

Mateo swung over, grabbing a new hold, and then continued upward.

Finally, he made it and rang the bell.

I remembered this well. Honing my strengths, building muscle memory, and pushing myself to the point I thought I'd black out. It had become a new outlet for me all those years ago. This was a physical exertion I enjoyed, and in part, was made for. Although these men were human, they were no less impressive with their ability to command their bodies.

This would become a new routine for them, and for me and Raif. Even my family would have to endure the change.

ON THE FIRST day of autumn, I sat outside headquarters on the stone wall. The sun's strength dwindled, although it still held some warmth of the summer. Enough that my skin turned red and my freckles darkened.

I turned at the sound of footsteps, and Sabrina plopped down next to me on a rock.

"You finally have an assignment should you want to take it," Sabrina said, holding up a paper in her hand.

My eyes widened as I took the paper, flipping it open. "Has it really been that quiet lately that this is the first to come in for me?"

Sabrina shrugged. "For you, yes. Not the first to come in in weeks, but per your criteria, things have been slim pickings for you." She paused and nodded toward the paper. "A known poacher targeted a family, and they for a fact know it was him because he boasted about it."

I kept my eyes trained on the paper, despite wanting

to know if the muscles in her face tightened or her eyes narrowed when she recited the information. If her voice was anything to go by, she didn't care, but when I finally glanced up at her, she quirked a brow.

"Does this appeal to you?"

Maybe she expected another reaction from me, but all I did was smile. Details were written down—where he lived, who he lived with, and something I hadn't been anticipating: how he should die. That was new. Normally, it was up to us how it happened. "They dictated how they want him to die?"

"It's new to me too, but I guess they want to feel as though they're living vicariously through a killer. Since they can't do it themselves."

"I'll do it." This assignment couldn't be personal, yet how could I remove myself entirely from the situation? If I took it personally, the outcome would be the same: this fucker would be dead.

Zeroing in on the date of the assignment, I lifted my eyes and laughed.

"What do you find so funny?"

"It's on my birthday." I was born in autumn, when the best apples were ripe, when the leaves were at their peak foliage and a hint of the first frost teased the air.

"Is that a problem?" There was a hint of a challenge in her tone, and she arched a brow.

"Not at all. It's just a unique present, I guess."

"Happy birthday," she offered dryly.

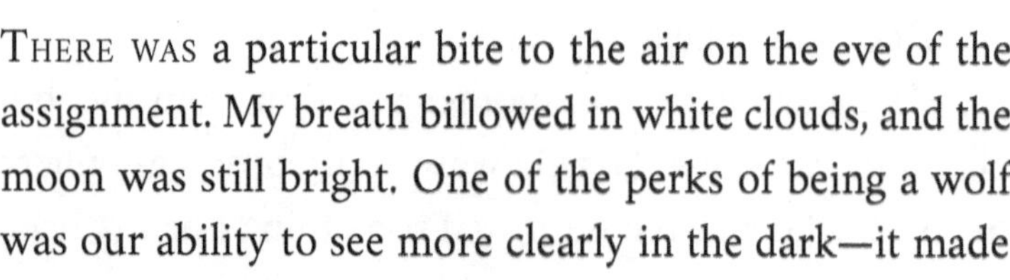

THERE WAS a particular bite to the air on the eve of the assignment. My breath billowed in white clouds, and the moon was still bright. One of the perks of being a wolf was our ability to see more clearly in the dark—it made us the ultimate predator, and in this case, only aided in my ability to take this poacher out.

It was amusing that the individual who'd sought out the hit had done his recon for us. They had followed the mark, watched his every move, and learned his habits enough to know what he'd be doing at this time of night.

Outside, next to the barn, my target filled a bucket of water for the livestock. He muttered something to himself as he walked inside, and I waited. The animals would give my presence away—wolves unnerved them —and I had no desire to give him a head start. I waited until he was done filling the trough.

Launching from the cover of the bushes, I rushed forward just as his body twisted to dump a barrel. A flash of silver in the moonlight caught his attention, but it was too late as I jabbed it into his side. He groaned, swore, and twisted to face his attacker with a scowl.

He wasn't slow, not as he came to his senses and rounded on me. His fist connected with my ribs, forcing the air from my lungs. If I had been foolish enough to leave the blade in his side, he would have used it on me, but I had no intention of offering him a weapon.

Drawn out—that was what the contract had said. He wanted this drawn out, and he wanted the man to suffer. I could do that. I could give the client that peace of mind.

I slid low, low enough that my dagger pierced his pants and bit into the back of his leg, right near a precious artery.

"You little s—" he began to curse at me but stopped as he barreled forward. I used his momentum to pull him to the ground, keeping my own weight low and centered.

The scent of his blood wafted in the air, his movements were slowing, and I used this opportunity to leap on him. He was too focused on one blade in my hand to realize there was a twin until that one nicked an artery in his arm. One nick at a time, he would bleed out, slowly and surely. After years of butchering, I knew exactly how deep to cut. Human flesh was not so different from a pig's hide.

He grabbed my hands, trying to use his brute strength to cause me to drop the blades, but Sabrina had killed the nerves there during training. Time after time, my knuckles collided with tree bark until the pain in them dulled. I may not have understood then, but I certainly did now.

When he managed to dislodge me, he grabbed ahold of my ankle. His grip tightened, and I knew what he wanted—to break it.

Quickly, I twisted around, my other foot connecting with his face, and as he began to retaliate, my tendons stretched painfully. With no other option, I twisted forward, moving my hand downward before I could think better of it. Somewhere, I must have actually thought it through, to adhere to the contract, because as the blade penetrated the flesh at the back of his neck, I twisted it, and his movements ceased at once. But he did not die. A skill I'd picked up through my many hits: figuring out what nerves to sever without killing my target.

"You bastard," he said, wide eyed. His voice was already losing its strength. Soon, he'd bleed out. "I can't . . . I can't feel my hands. My legs!"

Withdrawing the knife, I dragged it down his chest, and he sputtered but was unable to stir. The tip of the blade halted right above where his pancreas would be. I'd studied my fair share of anatomy to know where the best lethal wounds could be made. "And, because I want to make sure no one finds you alive—not that they'd be able to reverse your paralysis, but I suppose you could live—I'm going to ensure you die even if you're found." I paused and glanced down at his shirt. "Oh, how could I forget?"

I grabbed the hem of his shirt, then tore a piece off before balling it up into a wad. His screams would only bring attention, and that was the last thing I wanted. His head shook, and he almost turned it to the side but couldn't quite make it. He wouldn't open his mouth for me, so I squeezed his cheeks until he did and jammed the fabric in.

"Now, where were we . . . Ah, yes." I lifted the dagger again, pressing the blade into the flesh right over his pancreas, and then plunged it downward until there was a distinct pop. I quickly withdrew it, and blood bubbled out. The man screamed, but it was muted by the torn shirt. "This wound, it'll bleed quite profusely, but it's the pancreas' fluids that break your body down even if your wound happens to clot." I patted his leg and wiped the dagger free of his blood. "Maybe you ought to pray with the little breath you have left, if you believe in that sort of thing." I gave him one last look, secured my blades, and headed off into the woods with a limp.

It was late by the time I hobbled back to headquarters and went straight to the study. My ankle was furious with me. Sabrina sat waiting in a leather chair, her blue eyes taking in the limp, the dirt and blood. "Sit, now," she ordered and stood from her chair. She grabbed a towel, some herbs, and made her way to me. "Are you getting rusty?"

I chuckled and regretted it as my ribs complained. "No. I'm doing better than the mark."

She unlaced my boot unceremoniously and rolled my pant leg up so she could access the injury. Bruised, throwing off heat, and definitely ugly. She wrinkled her nose and emitted a hiss.

"He wrenched it, that's all."

"He didn't get you anywhere else?" she asked as her

fingers probed the area. After she was done assessing me, she lathered the herbal remedy on the swollen area.

"My back and ribs," I offered and propped my leg up when she prompted me with her hand.

"Let me see your back." She waited expectantly, and I groaned with the effort it took to strip my shirt off.

She hissed at the sight of my new bruises but didn't say anything as she rubbed the salve over my back, then my sides. The cool numbness spread over my muscles rather quickly.

"You're staying the night. I'll have Lukas run a note over to your family so they don't panic," she offered.

I had no energy left to disagree. So I curled up in the chair as best as I could and let darkness overtake me.

NINE

Someone plopped down next to me, rousing me from my sleep. My joints complained as I stretched, and the light streaming in through the window burned my eyes. The scent of baked apple wafted into the room, promptly waking my stomach.

Raif lifted a plate to me, and I took it, greedily shoving the pastry into my mouth.

I needed more than just a pastry, but humans were odd—they could eat dessert for breakfast, whereas us wolves preferred hardier things such as schlackwurst, bacon, pretzels, and jam.

"How's your ankle?" he signed.

"Feels better. I wouldn't run to the city on it, but I'd walk." It still hurt, but it wasn't swollen any longer.

"I have to go out tonight, wish me luck," he signed with a silent chuckle.

This was far from his first foray into the field. Raif

and Kina had been a part of the Huntsmen since I joined.

"Very little of the act has anything to do with luck, Raif. Be careful, be smart." I sighed. The streusel was hardly enough to touch the pit that was my stomach.

"Was it like riding a horse?" Raif signed.

I snorted. "Something like it. Muscle memory kicks in, then instinct, and before you know it, your work is done."

Long ago, any hint of remorse I may have felt was buried. My first hit, I hadn't been nervous, I hadn't stumbled, just sprang into action, relied on my training, and killed the man who had slain his wife amid a fight.

The mark I had last night? He was *bad* and could have eventually hunted *me*, or worse, my family.

Raif drank in what I said and looked out the window. "You should head home," he signed.

I nodded and leaned forward with a groan before tugging my boots on. When I stood, I tested my ankle and decided to lace that boot tighter so it would support me better.

Raif looked lost in his own world. Perhaps he was wondering about tonight, or maybe he was worried. Who could say? I knew he'd pull through, and more than that, I knew he'd go above and beyond. No one who was *that* meticulous while crafting could be sloppy when it came to other aspects in their life.

"Go home, Nik." He jerked his head, staring at me with those intense green eyes. "Home." He repeated the motion and let his fingers linger by his cheek.

"Yeah, yeah, I'm leaving." And I did and didn't bother to look back. As it was, everyone was probably worried about me.

Lu was outside when I arrived home. His back was to me as he hoisted a slaughtered pig up. Not just any pig but the damnable boar that loathed me. *Serves you right.* When Lu heard the crunch of leaves beneath my boot, he turned around, lines of concern etched on his face.

"Your sister and mother were worried about you," he said, turning his blue eyes away. It was his way of saying he was too.

"Lukas left you a note? I couldn't walk home last night." Assuming he read it, Lukas had told a half-truth —I hurt my ankle in the woods while helping them cut down a few trees and had to stay the night. But by the time Lukas had reached the house, it was too late to knock.

"Yeah," he grunted, scratching at his cheek. "Still, you've been spending an awful lot of time with them. Is everything okay?"

"Yeah, it's healing fast." I felt bad for lying, especially when it came from a place of caring, but he couldn't know, would never know. None of my family could know about what I did.

He nodded, then turned back to the pig.

Good talk, as always. I pushed my way into the house. The scent of minced meat pie made my mouth water at once, and when I stepped into the kitchen, I was bombarded with memories. A redhead stood at the stove with her hair in a bandana, humming a song, and I could have sworn it was my mother, but it wasn't.

"Figured the smell of pie would bring you home," Liesel snipped, not bothering to look at me as she took the pie out of the oven. It went without saying that I wasn't to touch it. That was our mother's rule, and it was now hers.

I shrugged, smirking. "You got me there."

"Well, since you weren't really around yesterday, I didn't get to tell you." She slanted me a half-hearted scowl. "Today Princess Stasya is visiting Bromiel—"

"As in, she's touring? For what reason, and why Bromiel?" It just so happened to be the neighboring town and one that was known for being the poorest in the country. Everyone knew about Bromiel because when someone mentioned they were from there, people frowned, and pity glimmered in their eyes.

"If you'd let me finish . . . yes, apparently the king wants her to grow used to visiting her people if she is to be crowned queen one day." This time, she did look at me, hope daring to spark in her eyes.

Thoughts ran rampant through my mind. If I could get there and speak to her privately without guards lingering around, perhaps there was a better chance at one of the royals listening. I hadn't forgotten my promise of returning to the castle or trying to convince the king to change his mind. However, I'd been busy with the huntsmen.

Liesel turned to look at me, her pale face full of concern. "That's good, right? Another chance to make a difference?"

"Maybe," I said quietly because I didn't know. There was something about Stasya that set her apart from her family and maybe that would work in our favor. I plopped down into a chair at the table and sighed.

The memory of Princess Stasya's clover-green eyes sprang to mind, and the way her white brows furrowed in warning—or maybe frustration.

"Well, eat up before you go. The Seidels have human stomachs, and with all the work you've been doing, you need real food." She grabbed a hunk of bread and smoked sausage that hung on the counter and deposited them on the table. "Tell me everything when you get back. I have to run to Nimblewick's." Liesel kissed the top of my head and flitted out of the kitchen.

Left alone, I devoured half the loaf of bread, a slice of the pie, and two links of sausage. With a full belly, I ventured back outside to our barn.

More often than not, I wished for a day that I could safely shift into a wolf and run to my destination without worrying if I'd be shot. Our draft horse, Brutus, was used to my presence and so didn't startle as I stepped up to his stall. He stuck his blond head over his door and sniffed the air, ears pricked forward as he waited for a treat. His unruly ivory mane covered one of his dark brown eyes.

After grabbing a handful of oats, I offered them to him, and he greedily ate. "We're going for a little ride today." Brutus nipped at his bridle hanging from his door, anticipating the trek. I took the bridle and opened the stall. He knew to bow his head so I could reach him, and then I slid the leather over his face, carefully positioning the bit so it didn't clang against his teeth.

"Time to go, old friend," I said, leading him out of the stall, then hoisted myself onto his bare back and urged him into a canter.

The surrounding forest was so thick that the sun scarcely shone through the treetops. It didn't matter that leaves were beginning to fall and pepper the ground; the evergreens grew close enough together that they blotted out the light. Even in the middle of Bromiel, the sun seemed to shy away, which gave it a macabre vibe. As if it wasn't dark enough, several smokestacks from nearby buildings expelled smoke, and whatever light may have filtered through the treetops seemed to be extinguished.

Typically, the streets were barren, but today they were lively. No doubt the townsfolk were attempting to create the perception they were better off. A good part of the population suffered. I'd known a few who drank themselves to death, and never attempted to move away, as if they were cursed to live and die on the soil they loathed.

Brutus clopped down the road, jigging when people grew too close to him.

"She's here!" a young girl shouted, perhaps only a year or two younger than Liesel.

Dragging my eyes toward the approaching carriage, I made the decision to hop down from my horse and walk him closer. The crowd was more willing to move for a giant horse than me.

Stasya's carriage was flanked by guards, which would have made it impossible to move in close enough to speak to her—but now wasn't the time anyway.

I led Brutus to a hitching post, though I was hesitant to do so—what if the princess bolted? What if someone had planned an assault? I quickly tied my horse up, then pushed my way through the crowd, daring anyone to retaliate.

Just as I stepped forward, Princess Stasya emerged from the carriage, her pale head bowed as a guard helped her down. Instead of having a cape wrapped around her shoulders, she wore a sleeveless maroon dress that dipped low enough to show off the valley between her breasts. "Thank you," she murmured demurely and cast her otherworldly eyes on the crowd before her. She searched it as if looking for someone and finally settled on a small girl in front. "Hello." She offered her hand in greeting and looked at the troubling sight before her.

The houses here were built mostly out of sticks and

resembled shacks, unlike the cottages in Walddorf. They were rickety and were a testament to how much the people were in need of assistance.

"Watch it," a man grumbled as I crept forward.

I slid my gaze toward him and offered a glare. He muttered an obscenity but backed away.

Stasya, still surrounded by guards, was led down the row of buildings, listening to the townsfolk speak to her plainly of what required the most work, what they thought would help the state of their town and people.

I knew this because, like everyone else, I followed her like a sheep on the heels of their shepherd.

"I believe if people knew how much lumber we had to offer, then perhaps they'd seek us out rather than a town farther away or even outside of Abendrot! It would help the town and bring light to it once more in so many ways," an older woman offered, her worn fingers gnarled and wrinkled.

That was one of their many issues: they had resources, but no one paid them any heed because . . . well, because it was Bromiel.

"We have so many trees to offer, surely we could establish sawmills. We have talented woodworkers if only people would remember us."

I grimaced. It was sad to hear the desperation in their voices, and to Stasya's credit, she didn't school her face into an unreadable mask. No, she let her concern and consideration wash over her face—as if she were truly listening to their plight.

The crowd grew thicker, which made the guards

tighten their security and made me consider the surroundings. A butcher was rendering fat in the front of his shop, the scent permeating the air. There were so many people around, it wouldn't take much to cause a distraction.

I crept closer to the cauldron of fat and *accidentally* bumped into it. The pot, which had been balancing precariously over an iron grate, tipped over, and flames erupted, following the river of grease.

Not the brightest idea. I leaped out of the way as fire spread rapidly. The crowd panicked, pushing the guards back, creating a lapse in the protective circle around Stasya. I seized the moment, bolting forward and grabbing her.

She cried out, beating against me as I ushered her through the writhing mob of people, and the guards, for the moment, had no idea I'd taken her.

Stasya thrashed in my grasp violently, but I easily hoisted her up to avoid kicks to my shins. Screaming, she flailed harder, trying to capture the attention of her guards, yet they couldn't hear a damn thing over the cries of the people as they threw dirt over the fire to contain it.

Thrusting her into a vacant hut, I slammed the door shut and slid the wooden plank down to lock it. She rammed into me, punching my bruised ribs. Balling my hands into fists, I turned on her and snarled, "Stop!" She came at me again. This time, I grabbed her by the wrists and pinned them down to her sides.

Stasya pushed back, surprising me with how strong she was. Still, she couldn't free herself of my hold.

"I'm not going to hurt you." In response to my words, she kicked my shin, and I had half a mind to tie her up so she would stop flailing.

"Really?" she spat out and looked down at my hands around her wrists. When she lifted her gaze, recognition must have dawned on her.

At the same time, I realized what I'd sensed at the castle. What set her apart from her family, what *drew* me to her. "You're . . ."

Wolf.

"Don't say it," she snapped, scowling at me.

I didn't have to say it. Releasing her, I laughed at the irony of it all and only ceased chuckling when I felt the cold sting of a slap against my face. Shaking it off, I turned my full attention to her. "Well, princess, I'm not. I've decided I'm not giving your family a third chance to change the way this kingdom is ruled. For too long, the wolves have been hunted and nothing has been done about it. This was *our* kingdom first, and it was only because your grandfather *murdered* King Vanhal that the humans ever inherited the throne." A snarl ripped from me, and before I knew it, I had backed her up against the side of the hut.

To her credit, she didn't back down. Instead, she growled right back. "I am not to blame. And believe me, I understand the plight and wish to do something about it, but do you think for one moment my father would allow for that?"

"So you're in agreement that he's allowing this to happen?"

"Of course I am! Do you believe I enjoy standing by as families are torn apart? He hates wolves, so if you have any attachment to your head, you'll stay *away*!"

I flexed my fingers, the scent of Stasya invading every one of my senses. She smelled like fresh-cut flowers on a late spring day. Coupled with her pheromones, it was mouthwatering.

Focusing on what she'd said, I shook my head. "Your father is a hypocrite." When she started to cut in, I lifted my hand. "No. Let me finish. He is a hypocrite because he has no qualms about using wolves to aid him but thinks nothing of their deaths."

"What do you mean? He doesn't *use* them." Stasya's brows furrowed in confusion, and she crossed her arms, drawing my attention to her creamy breasts.

"Gregor."

She drew her head back. "How do you know about him?"

"He's my sire." I hated claiming him, but if I had any hope of reaching Stasya, I had to form a connection with her somehow.

Her mouth formed an O, but she didn't say anything, not as she reassessed me. What did she see, I wondered? Gregor and I shared so many similarities, except he was darker in every way.

"What is your name?"

I could have given her the moniker I'd chosen. It would have been the smart thing to do. But I was here to reason with her. And she now knew what Gregor was to me, so it would be easy enough to connect the dots. "Niklaus."

"Niklaus," she echoed, and for some reason, my name on her lips stirred heat in my belly that had nothing to do with the moon's pull.

Something else. Although I didn't want to wonder what that was.

"Answer me this, Stasya . . . if you're a wolf and his personal guard is too, why hasn't he stopped the mass murders once and for all?"

Stasya sat down in a rickety wooden chair and ran her hands over her rosy cheeks. "He hates them too much. He loves me, but his hatred runs deep because of what happened to me." I didn't press for more, but I assumed that she had been bitten at some point in her life. "And Gregor . . . He was my father's guard long before he knew that he was a werewolf, and when he discovered that Gregor was, he didn't care. Because at the end of the day, Gregor protects him."

Just a loyal hound. Except, Gregor was loyal to no one except for himself.

Still, something had to be done. Something had to change, and if it took me rattling Ansgar, so be it. "Return home and speak with him, or I will, and you won't like how I do it. Or maybe I'll talk to Edda." No part of me liked bringing her sister into it, but if I had to . . .

"Do not say her name." A growl rumbled in her chest, and she looked poised to launch herself at me.

I was certain the only thing that kept her rooted where she was was the etiquette that had likely been drilled into her skull since childhood. There was something rather intriguing about Stasya: the elegant angles of her face, the way she held her lips. Something twisted inside my chest, and I realized she captivated me.

Ansgar didn't deserve a third chance, but Stasya did.

I crossed the distance between us and tilted her chin back. There was a large part of me that wanted to undo the crown braid and thread my fingers in her hair, watch it tumble down her bare back.

Irritated with myself, I glanced to the side, collecting my thoughts once more. "I'll give you a month, only a month, before I come knocking for the third and last time," I said.

"You can't—"

Guards shouted outside, searching for Stasya, and as she moved her head, I reached out to wrap a loose lock of her pale hair around my finger. Silvery as the full moon. "Has it always been this color?" I asked, transfixed by her once again.

She pulled away, still uncertain if I was going to harm her, and I couldn't blame her. "No, it changed. I was blond when I was a girl."

"Before you were bitten?" I asked bluntly. Werewolves were born, no different than a human, but they could also infect a human with their bite on a full moon.

It wasn't hard to deduce, and the way she glared before her green eyes softened told me I had hit the mark. She looked as though she was contemplating telling me. This was, at least, an upgrade from wanting to claw my face off. "Yes. One strand at first, and then several others. In a year's time, it was silver."

"It suits you."

Her expression soured as she looked at me. "Unless you want to be stabbed, I suggest you open that door and let me go. We're done here."

"If I open that door, I *will* be stabbed." Upon entering the hut, I had searched for the routes we could use, and the window toward the back yard would suffice. "We'll use the window."

TEN

"I won't go through that window, it'll tear my dress." She moved her hand toward the skirt. It draped over her legs like a second skin. It wasn't meant for much more than walking, and the fabric, if I wasn't mistaken, was silk.

I clucked my tongue and offered a hand. "I could always help you out of it."

"Excuse you!" she cried out, slapping my hand away.

"Do you have a better idea?" Stepping back, I glanced around the small hovel for another point of exit. There was nothing.

"No," she huffed.

"So, which is it: ripping the dress or stripping to your underthings?"

Red rushed into Stasya's ears, painting her cheeks scarlet and making her eyes seem all the brighter.

"Would it make you feel better to know I've seen

plenty of naked females?" Probably not. I bit my tongue, wondering why I'd said that.

She stared at me incredulously. "No."

"Normally, seeing another wolf naked is commonplace. We run together, shift together, and there is little care whether or not you see one another's d—body parts."

Her cheeks had turned so red that she matched the hue of her dress. "I wasn't raised that way."

Fair enough. "So, have you decided which option you'd like?" I glanced toward the window. The guards were closing in, their voices getting louder, and the sound of their boots neared.

"I need to finish this tour, and I am not doing that with a torn dress." I supposed that was the closest Stasya would get to asking me to undress her.

She stood and turned her back to me. The dress laced up and needed more effort to loosen it. We didn't have much time to spare.

I stepped closer, dragging my fingers along her smooth skin, I'd considered ripping the back entirely, but I'd been raised better than that. I loosened what I could, but we didn't have the luxury of time on our side. Toward the end, I tore the last few away.

Stasya gasped. "You said you'd undo my dress, not rip it!" She held the fabric against her chest, but even still, I could see the crimson spilling into her cheeks.

"Listen, princess, I wasn't trying to. Otherwise, you'd only have a rag left." A thought occurred to me. "Hand over the dress. I'll give it back in a moment." She kept her back to me but did as I said. I walked to the hearth, where glowing embers puffed small clouds of smoke. I dipped the skirt into the embers, waiting until it caught fire, and watched the flames lick and devour several inches. Satisfied, I stomped on it and returned to Stasya's side.

"It'll look like you caught fire," I explained as she quirked a brow in question. With her back facing me, the smoothness of her skin teased my eyes, and my cock hardened because I chose that moment to think about Stasya revealing herself to me inch by inch.

My eyes slid from her ankles, up her toned legs, to her slender backside then to the milky skin of her back.

Stasya sucked in a breath, and I wondered what she thought—felt. Did she feel that inexplicable pull too?

"Are you ready?" I asked hoarsely and pulled away, forcing myself not to watch her as she moved. I waited by the window and kept my eyes lowered as she approached, although I wanted very much to thoroughly assess her every curve.

Pushing open the window, I climbed out first and helped Stasya through as well. She stumbled into my chest, lingering there as her eyes met mine. If I hadn't been this close, I would have missed her pupils change— widen. I smelled the subtle change in the air as her arousal teased me, and my gut twisted.

Arousal?

Stasya caught herself and stumbled back, clutching her dress to her body.

"For a moment, I thought you were going for my jugular," I said, trying my best to alleviate the tension.

Her head jerked in my direction, a quizzical expression on her face. "What?"

"I'm just saying, you looked poised to bite."

"No," she said breathlessly, blinking rapidly.

We were running out of time and as much as I wanted to inquire as to what the hell that had been all about, we needed to move. Bending down, I scooped up some dirt, and while Stasya wasn't paying attention, I rubbed it on her cheeks and arms quicker than she had time to react.

She huffed again and looked down at the filth in disgust. "Really?"

"Gotta make it look convincing. There is a pig slop over there if you feel so inclined to roll in it?"

"You are disgusting . . ."

"Now or never . . ." I leaned in closer to her, our lips inches apart, and her face twisted into the most sumptuous scowl I had ever seen in my life. "I'm here to rescue the princess," I rumbled.

Stasya cursed under her breath, which surprised me, but then she ran her fingers through her hair, mussing it up.

I supposed she wanted to look as though she'd been through quite the ordeal, but with the scent of her still-present desire hanging in the air between us, she appeared thoroughly rumpled, and it made me want to push her back through that window and see what happened next.

"Alric, over here," she shouted, tearing me from my thoughts.

The harried guard rushed over, glancing between the two of us.

I lifted my hands in surrender. "I found her like this." Stasya merely nodded.

"Your Highness, you're—" Alric stammered, averting his gaze, and then locked eyes with me. "You—"

I wondered for a moment if Stasya would turn against me. I'd snatched her from the safety of her guards, threatened her, and ripped her dress from her. If the roles had been reversed, I don't know that I'd have bitten my tongue.

Stasya glanced over at me, then to her approaching guard. "Alric, thankfully this villager found me. My skirt caught flame, and he pulled me aside to extinguish it. Unfortunately, my dress—" She glanced down at the tattered heap of fabric in her grasp, a blush blooming across the bridge of her nose. "I am grateful that he was able to offer me aid."

She owed me nothing, and though we didn't have the time nor the moment to discuss matters further, I believed that her heart ached for the werewolves in Abendrot. And maybe she had been waiting for someone like me to bring change.

Maybe.

Alric remained quiet, then gave me a curt nod. That was as close to as a "thank you" as I'd be getting from him. I winked at the guard and turned my gaze toward

Stasya, mouthing "one month" to her before I slipped into the calming crowd.

In one month, I'd be visiting the royals again, and if nothing had been done, *something* would be done. If I had to prove a point to light a fire beneath the ass of the king, then I'd do it. One wolf did not paint all of them bad, and I had a feeling there was more to Stasya's story. While it was none of my business to know it, perhaps it'd clarify things, mostly as to why her father hated *all* of them so much that he would sit on his hands while hundreds of lives were lost every year, but especially as of late.

WHEN BRUTUS and I returned home, Lu was in the barn cleaning the stalls. He leaned on his pitchfork, his gaze following us as I led the horse back to his stall.

"What came of Bromiel?"

I snorted. "Chaos? There was a fire, and it derailed the princess' visit for a time. I didn't stay long enough for the whole ordeal." While true, Lu didn't need to know about my personal chat with Stasya. "I doubt anything will come of the tour, but we will see. One way or another, I believe change is in the wind." Of course, I knew this because I'd be doing something about it. I was done lingering in the shadows.

Lu nodded. "Good enough, I guess."

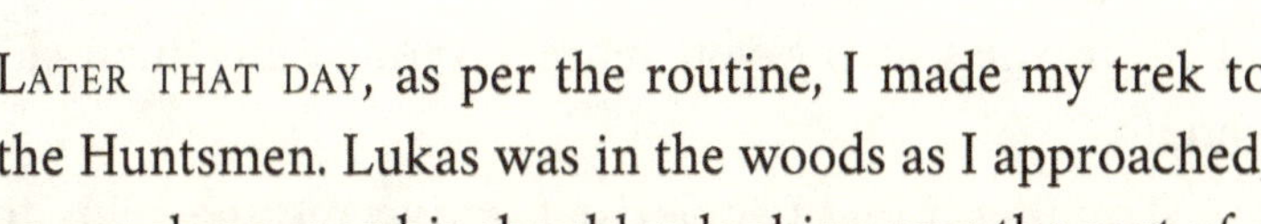

LATER THAT DAY, as per the routine, I made my trek to the Huntsmen. Lukas was in the woods as I approached, an axe slung over his shoulder, looking ever the part of a lumberjack.

"How nice of you to show up," he griped.

"I have a life outside of the Huntsmen too. While detaching from society may apply to the new recruits, it wasn't on my contract with you." What would I have done if it had been? Turn my back on my mother, my sister, and Lu?

Unlikely.

Lukas swung the axe over his head and brought it down onto an awaiting log. It split in two and fell to the side. "Grab some of the logs and carry them in with me." He motioned to follow him.

I bent and piled a stack of wood in one arm, then followed Lukas as he led the way with an armful as well.

"Sometimes I forget you can just shut your mouth and follow an order."

"Although difficult, it isn't impossible," I quipped.

Lukas opened the door to the cabin and filed in. I followed. He brought the wood to the massive hearth next to the stairs and dropped his armful, then motioned for me to do the same.

Once my arms were free of logs, I stood and brushed

my hands off on my pants. Lukas' brow furrowed. He always seemed to have a frown, but today it seemed more apparent.

He grunted. "Sabrina trusts you, and while I do too . . . I think she's giving you more responsibility than she should."

"Training a few people isn't giving me the reins to the operation, Lukas," I replied dryly.

"There just . . . Seven years you've been here, but there is something I feel as though you aren't telling us."

This was the moment when I could have told him what I was. That the reason I took to hunting people down so easily was that I was a natural-born hunter. I was a natural-born werewolf, driven by instincts.

I didn't. I couldn't.

The secret went beyond me; it went to Liesel and Mama too.

I needed to protect them.

"Maybe you're paranoid, Lukas." I shrugged. "Unless you want to know about my first wet dream?"

The comment earned me a cold glare, but surprisingly, nothing more. No punch to the shoulder or a slap upside the head, which would have been more along the lines of what usually transpired between us.

Was this really bothering Lukas that much?

"There is nothing that would harm the Huntsmen or Sabrina." He seemed to relax at the latter part.

"We all have secrets, but I just ask that yours never bring hellfire on us. Understand?"

Fair enough.

With a nod, I ventured into the training room, where the three recruits and Raif waited. He turned to me, his lips twisting with annoyance—at me for being late—then he signed.

"Team up," Raif said, and I echoed his movements with my voice.

Kranz and Mateo paired up, which left Breck as the odd one out. Raif crossed the room to stand next to him.

"We are solitary workers, but we must know how to work with a partner too. So we'll work through a few routines." Without so much as a word, I turned on Kranz and Mateo, ducking low and sweeping my leg toward Mateo's. I was too quick, and he wasn't ready, so he landed hard on his ass, but Kranz was already advancing on me, lashing out with his leg to kick me backward.

I rolled aside, spun onto my knees, and reached for Kranz's ankle. With a yank, he crashed to the floor, but Mateo was charging toward me.

So the dance went until I exhausted Kranz and Mateo.

They hadn't managed a successful hold on me because they'd each been too busy focusing on outdoing the other or using the techniques they'd learned. Sometimes, it was about throwing that out the window and seeing what was in front of you.

I drank in air greedily, controlling my breaths. Sweat trickled down my back, dripped down my chin. "Now, face off with the other team, and try to use what you learned just then."

Just as the words left my mouth, Lukas cleared his throat from the doorway. I walked up to him and lifted a brow. "What is it?"

"Tonight, you'll be visiting Amschteg." He waved a letter—an assignment. "Go clean up and change your clothing. I'll tell you more of it after."

I headed inside and to the changing room, where my black attire awaited me. Black boots, pants, and a long-sleeved shirt with a half-mask sewn into the neck. When in place, it slid to cover everything beneath my eyes.

My clothes would have to wait. For now, I had to scrub the blood and grime from my face and hands. Against the wall was a wash basin with a bar of soap and cloth. I scrubbed away, getting as much dirt off of me as possible, then turned to get dressed. Although I wasn't certain what tonight would call for, I opted for twin blades and sheathed them on either side of my hips.

After I was ready, I sought Sabrina out in her study. She sat reclined in her chair, poring over a paper in her grasp. A moment ticked by, then she glanced up at me. "Amschteg, as you heard. The dishonorable Lord Gustaf Pinzer has a bad habit of dabbling with young girls." She eyed me pointedly, and I arched a brow. "Yes, exactly what you're thinking."

Disgusting. If anyone deserved to be taken out of this life, it was people like Gustaf. "Are there any specific requests for this one?"

"None. Get creative. The pay is a surprise."

"You mean it's a freebie," I offered dryly.

"Quite the opposite . . . I mean it's more than we've

seen come through here before. I'll surprise you with the figure once you've made it back."

"The timeframe?"

"None. You can be home for supper if you'd like."

"Living arrangements?" There had to be some information on him. I wasn't going to walk in without some knowledge of his lifestyle.

"Alone. He's sixty years old, no kin and no wife. He terrorizes his female staff and frequently disturbs the ones at court affairs." Sabrina pinched the bridge of her nose and sighed. "Just do what you're good at."

Killing.

She slid a piece of paper across the desk, then leaned back in the chair. "Here are the coordinates to his mansion."

Coordinates? Typically, we had to perform recon ourselves because our clients were too afraid of being caught. Too afraid the paper trail would lead back to them.

Whoever put out a hit for Gustaf wasn't scared of being caught. They just wanted him dead.

Snatching up the paper, I glanced down at the address and snorted. "Fancy little twit, isn't he? Well, it's time he learned what it is to be terrorized and face judgment."

Eleven

Amschteg was opulent in comparison to the capital city. Whereas the capital housed the growing businesses and massive markets, Amschteg housed the wealth of the country. Often, I'd heard others describe it as a pristine town, but it was all a farce. This place might have looked as if it had been carved from a section of heaven, but the refuse lurked in the shadows.

Buildings stretched toward the sky and massive mansions sprawled across manicured lawns. Iron gates ensured that no wandering unsavories would be able to step foot on the green grass. It struck me as odd. Yesterday, I'd stood in the poorest town, and today, I stood in the richest.

Lord Pinzer's mansion, at first glance, was ostentatious. And at second glance, it was even more so. Brick upon brick was stacked for two stories until it met the next portion, which was timber painted white.

No one milled around his yard, and perhaps the gate would ward most people off, but I wasn't most people. Hopping the gate, I tugged the half-mask into place below my nose and strode toward the house. A young servant, not much older than Liesel, emerged from around the house. Her eyes widened as she caught sight of me, and as I lifted a finger to my mouth, she nodded her head, understanding in her gaze as I approached the back.

"Get him for us all," she whispered. "He's in his study." She shifted away but not before I was able to catch sight of her rounded belly.

"Like a wolf in the hen house, he is," said an older woman by her side, locking eyes with me.

"I'm not afraid of the Big Bad Wolf, not today," the younger one said, then disappeared down the hall.

The letter had specifically asked for The Big Bad Wolf to come and take out the wretched man. But to hear someone in close proximity use my moniker, it almost put a smile on my face. Both of the women sounded so relieved, it just drove me onward as I wound through the house.

It was quiet, and most of the other servants were occupied in their quarters. The scent of a pipe snaked its way through the hall toward me, and it only grew stronger as I grew closer to the study.

Gustaf was chuckling down at his desk, muttering something occasionally.

"You have a choice: easy way or hard way. Decide now." My hands hung by my sides, loose and yet ready to spring into action.

He startled, then blinked at me. "Who the bugger are you! And why are you in my house? I'm not giving you a dime, you wretched . . ." Gustaf leaned down, pulling free a small crossbow that must have been under his desk.

Before he had the chance to let loose an arrow, I dodged to the side. Not a moment later the arrow whizzed by my head, embedding itself into the wall. "I said, decide."

"Screw you." Gustaf rose and lumbered toward me.

"I was hoping you'd choose the harder way." As I unsheathed one of the daggers at my hip, Gustaf's eyes widened, but he seemed to think that this was a bluff, for he chuckled at me. "You're not going to kill me."

I wasn't bluffing, and I most certainly was going to kill him.

I drew out the movement and took him by surprise as I slammed the blade down onto his hand, pinning it to the table.

"And why wouldn't I? You're a greedy man and you can't keep your hands off your staff."

Blood seeped from the wound as he howled in pain, and spittle flecked his lips and chin as he panted. "You monster!"

"No, no, that is your title. You've been harassing enough women." I drew my next blade and sauntered toward him casually. "You're thoroughly finished." He'd never have another chance to sully another one of his servants. He'd never breathe again.

"I'll have your head for this, you have no idea who I am."

"Sure I do, Lord Gustaf. Owner of the bank of Amschteg, highly esteemed by King Ansgar . . . " I'd read more about him when Sabrina handed me the assignment papers.

"You don't think the king would notice my death? You're wrong. And he'll come for you." A mad laugh escaped him. Clearly he thought himself the victor in this.

"I am counting on him noticing. You see, I hope he gets the message that people like you need to disappear."

I relished the sound of his cries as he yanked the blade from his hand, the scent of his blood lingering in the room. Waving my dagger, I motioned toward the other in his grasp. "Are you going to use it on me, porky?"

"Damn right, I am," he hissed as he wrapped his kerchief around his hand quickly and came my way, charging like a boar intent on goring.

His blade went in for a blow, but my arm came down on his, and with my free hand, I twisted his arm around and lifted until I heard a satisfying pop.

Another cry rang out from Gustaf, and I relented only because I wanted to prolong this dance. As his limp arm dangled by his side and he panted heavily, I snatched the blade that was nearly falling out of his grasp.

"What else?" I teased.

"No more," he pleaded with me.

"Now, that . . . that is amusing because I'm sure you've heard that before."

And so it went for an hour, until the man was gurgling a pool of his own blood, rasping.

"Who are you?" Blood poured from his mouth.

The memory of the girl and woman roused, and I replied, "The Big Bad Wolf."

FOR A MONTH, it was one ruthless mission after the next, and the country began to whisper about the shadow known as the *Big Bad Wolf*. How he was a devil doing an angel's work. That part made me chuckle. Yet, despite the rumors circulating about me, the Stasya hadn't convinced the king to make any changes to the kingdom.

So, as I promised, I stood outside the castle, torches blazing to illuminate the structure even in the absolute dark. There was no moon this night, entirely absent, but the stars winked down silently, offering me all the light I needed.

All of the guards that were close enough for me to locate were human. I'd have smelled their otherness had they been wolf or witch. At least they wouldn't scent my arrival, which would make this easy—hopefully.

I pulled myself up the wall and ran a distance to where there was a gap in patrol, then let my form plummet ten feet down. I landed quietly and wove around to the vine-covered siding. The black clothing allowed me to move freely but also unseen even when the flames shifted and cast light on where I was.

Hopping through an open window, I took in the surroundings. It was the end of a hallway, no guards around this wing. There were several drapes hanging along the walls which could be used as cover as I advanced down the hall.

A familiar laugh bounced along the hall, and I quickly darted into a room. It didn't sound as if anyone was in it, but as I closed the door and spun around, I discovered I was wrong.

Edda.

Her mouth gaped open, and her throat worked as if she wanted to scream but couldn't find her voice to do so.

"No, shh, listen," I began, "I'm not here to hurt you." I wouldn't, but she didn't know that—especially in my current attire.

"What do you want?" she whispered softly. "My jewels are over there on my dresser. I don't have any coin on me."

"I don't want that." My eyes flicked to the door, and I planted a hand on it as footsteps neared.

"Edda? Can I come in?" Stasya called out. She didn't wait for her sister to reply and instead tried the door. "Edda, what are you doing?" she asked with a laugh.

Grumbling, I opened the door, yanked her inside, and brought a hand to her mouth. "Don't."

She jerked her head away from my hand. "You!" she spat out.

"I'd say it's a pleasure, but considering no advancements were made in a month, it isn't, is it?" Narrowing my eyes, I made no indication I was willing to move away from the door.

"Stasya, what does he want?" Edda asked worriedly.

"It's okay, Edda, he's not going to hurt you." She sent a fiery look in my direction. "You won't."

She was right about that; I wouldn't and had no desire to. But for my cause, I'd certainly pretend I had every intention of killing her.

"This is how it's going to go: you're both coming with me. Edda, you'll be in front of Stasya, and Stasya, you will be held hostage. We're going to pay your father a visit." My tone brooked no argument, especially as I unsheathed a long dagger from my hip. "Walk," I ordered.

Outside of the room, the girls moved without complaint—mostly. If Stasya could, she would have spit venom in my eyes, but when I brushed my thumb along her jaw, it was a reminder that while this may have been an act, I still had a blade against her neck. One wrong move on either of our parts and she would bleed.

"Lead the way."

"There are guards all over," she began. Edda turned to look back at us, and she huffed.

"They could very well grab Edda, but you, Stasya, are

the one being held." In fact, I wished they would grab Edda. For one, she didn't need to see this, even though it was all for theatrics. And two, I didn't doubt that she would wail for her sister, bringing more guards to the area and creating hysteria.

Stasya's hands clenched by her sides as if she was contemplating moving away or even trying to attack me, but even as she breathed, the blade pressed against her throat, and with the slightest pressure, a trickle of blood ran down her pale skin. She hissed as it did.

"I wouldn't."

"Fine."

Apparently, she wasn't fazed by the notion of being held hostage. "Simmer down, princess."

A sound of disgust came from her as we walked down the hall, and before long, a guard came into view. He cried out and rushed forward. My lips twisted behind the mask. "Don't. One wrong move, and she'll be dead." I cocked my head so my breath tickled at her ear.

Strangely, I felt her shudder against me, but it wasn't fear I scented. Turning my attention toward the shouts in the distance, I heard them order someone to hide the king away.

"No, don't. Let us talk to him," Stasya tried to reason with the guards, but they were not listening; they were trained to protect the king.

In the corridor, as we advanced down, Edda wandered forward a little too far, which allowed a guard to sweep her away from the danger. It would be easier this way.

"No, Stasya!" Edda cried out as they pulled her down the hall.

"Where is his room?" I asked her calmly.

"Down the hall to the left. You can't miss the carved oak doors. Would you loosen the blade?"

"Not happening. Move."

And she did. The guards were collecting, shouting orders, and servants froze in place as we made our way to the king's bedroom door. I kicked at the double doors, glaring at the engraved wood. Two wolves standing on a rocky cliff side, overlooking a stream. It struck me as odd that Ansgar, and his line, loathed wolves so much yet there still happened to be pieces of the werewolves *everywhere.* In the emblem, in the decor, the banner…

"Your Majesty . . . I think you'll want to open the door and let me in," I growled.

"Unlikely. Who are you?" he spat out. "How ever you got into my castle—"

"Is really of no consequence at this point. Let me in. Let. Me. In," I growled.

"Please, Father," Stasya pleaded with him.

The doors flew open. He stood in his nightdress and stumbled backward as he saw the severity of the situation. He didn't know it was staged and didn't know that I wouldn't hurt her. Of course, he *did* see the blood trickling down her throat, which sold the current situation all the better.

"Let her go!" His eyes widened, and he lifted a trembling hand. "At once, you let her go!"

"You're in no position to make demands."

The king glanced at the guards, who stood poised to attack but didn't dare as I held Stasya at knifepoint. "Do not advance on him!"

I jerked my head toward the room, and the king backed up, allowing me in. But I remained focused on the guards looming even as I walked into the king's quarters. I used my foot and kicked the door shut. One arm slid around the front of Stasya while I held the blade against her neck. "We have something to discuss."

"What, what could you possibly want to discuss?!"

"Werewolves."

A disgusted noise left him, and I felt the princess stiffen against me. "What of them?"

"Would you at least listen to him? This pertains to me as well."

"You are not a werewolf! You were attacked!" he spat out, lifting his hands as he grew enraged. "You were bitten by an infected handmaiden, it wasn't your fault."

"Neither was it theirs. I should have known better than to approach her, but I thought it was fascinating, and she turned on me. I never blamed her, but you killed her, and you've signed up thousands to die too."

"There is nothing I can do. I cannot call it off. I made a bargain, Stasya, and I cannot go back on it."

"A bargain?" Stasya murmured. "What are you talking about?" Somewhere along the way, I had let the blade drop from her neck and relaxed my hold on her. She didn't bother to move.

A moment later, guards pounded on the door. "Majesty! Do you want us to advance?"

They wanted to, no doubt, and their training required they did as much, but they didn't know whether or not I was about to gut the princess from stem to sternum.

Ansgar looked positively green around the gills. His face paled considerably, then he glanced to the side. "Remain outside!" He worked his jaw, then paced. I could nearly see the cogs turning in his mind. How could he get out of this? What could he say? Could he bargain with me?

"Father, what did you do?" Stasya pitched her voice low. "What did you do?!"

I stepped to the side, glancing between Stasya and Ansgar, not liking the direction this was heading. My skin prickled in apprehension for what he was to say next . . .

TWELVE

Stasya advanced on her father. "Tell me!" Her voice shook, but I wasn't certain if it was from fear or anger. Maybe it was both.

"Abendrot has lost favor with its alliances, and although we still have a few, they are dwindling. In a weak moment, I sought out someone whom I thought to be a true ally, but I didn't know that I would be in their pocket—that they'd have hidden and unreasonable terms—

"Vorhol had always been a reliable alliance. When I reached out for aid, I was put into contact with the king's councilman, the Hawk. I didn't know at the time that he had minions, whom he calls his flock." Ansgar slowly lowered himself to the edge of his mattress and sighed. "A few years back, the kingdom fell into even more financial trouble. We exceeded our spending limits, and we had no choice but to borrow from someone willing to loan us coin. The Hawk. He's a wealthy man . . ."

"That has nothing to do with wolves." And aside from how the finances of the kingdom affected everyone I knew, I didn't really care to hear about that. "I'm talking about half the population of Abendrot, the rightful heirs to the kingdom." When Ansgar said nothing, I added, "My mother nearly died because of you."

Stasya moved her head to look up at me, frowning, but said nothing.

"If she was a wolf, she deserved it." He sniffed haughtily, and that was all it took to send me after him.

Launching at him, I pushed his frame to the mattress. "I could end you here and now." I hissed the words as the need to protect my family, and Stasya too, flared to life. How could he dismiss his daughter so readily simply because of what she was?

"No! Please, no. Don't!" Stasya cried out. "Stop, Father!"

"It was part of the deal! I would grant the Hawk control of Abendrot and eventually a seat on the Council, and in turn, he'd help eradicate the werewolves, as well as provide the kingdom money."

There it was. An admission.

My hand worked its way around his neck, clamping down as he pawed at me to get off, but I was beyond reasoning with, and my vision was fading to black. Ansgar deserved to die for slaughtering so many, for being so careless when it came to his daughter.

Stasya shoved my shoulder and caused me to rock, but I was fully intent on killing him.

"Stop! Please!" Stasya yanked at my clothes, but I didn't want to relinquish my hold on him until he was dead. "Niklaus!" she shrieked.

The guards chose that moment to burst into the room, and they rushed toward the bed, swords drawn.

I relinquished my grip on the king and sprang from the bed, backing away toward his balcony door. "Call off your hounds, Ansgar, or you'll regret it."

Whether he was frightened enough or believed my words, he motioned for the guards to stand down. When they sheathed their swords, I relaxed a fraction.

Stasya blurted out her words. "I . . . I have a proposition. I want to hire you to take out the Hawk. If I do that, will this end? The werewolves being slain and the threats to me?"

Ansgar didn't respond, but then his eyes focused on me, and it was like watching a wick ignite. "Niklaus . . ." His eyes widened. "Gregor's son? He warned me about you." His eyes flicked to his guards. "Step outside the door for a moment." The guards reluctantly obeyed and left the room, but the doors remained open.

I growled. What did my sire have to say about me other than that I was his spawn? He knew me no more than a hole in the wall. "You should have listened, then." I glanced at Stasya. "If I agree—and that is a big if—will you swear on your daughter's life that you'll protect wolves from here on out?"

"I cannot. My deal has been struck with the Hawk."

Absolute imbecile. Not only trading a kingdom but the lives of half its population? I nodded. "Then you forfeit your daughter's life. Who is to say that one day, one of those birds won't come after her?" In his delusional mind, the king likely considered his daughter set apart from the society of wolves, but she was one of us, and if he valued her life as he said, he would obey.

King Ansgar's bottom lip wobbled as he mulled over the facts. "What have I done?" he murmured and covered his face.

"Will you swear on her life?" I prompted him.

"Yes." He slid his gaze toward her. "You must believe I never meant for you to be in harm's way . . ."

Stasya looked utterly drained. She sighed and shook her head. "I know, but I am a wolf. It's your mission to punish a race that isn't to blame. Yes, a werewolf bit me, but I am not bitter. Why should you be?"

For this, Ansgar didn't have the words. "I am frightened. Somehow, the Hawk has found out your truth. He sent me a missive, and he knows. He knows what you are, and if I should go back on our agreement, he will have your life as payment, Stasya."

Shaking beside me, Stasya's green eyes hardened. "How?!"

"I can only guess someone in the castle must have relayed it. I don't know what to do. Who to trust." His voice shook, and if I'd thought he was pale before, he was even more so now.

Stasya looked to me, stricken. "How do I finalize the contract?" she asked.

To finalize a contract, there had to be payment, and I didn't want money from the crown. I'd sooner toss it into the sea. What I wanted was true freedom for my kind, including Stasya. "I will take your freedom as payment."

"You wretched . . ." The king moved forward as if to attack me, and I wished he would so I could throw him to the floor.

My lips twisted in mild amusement. "I am not the one who unwittingly placed a hit on my kin, am I? If not her freedom, then her life, but not as you think."

"What the devil do you even mean by that?" Ansgar stammered.

In Bromiel, I had seen it flitter across her face, had seen the way her pupils blew wide in my presence, and although I wasn't the best when it came to tuning into another's emotions, there was a tug whenever I was in Stasya's presence. One that felt *natural*.

Sabrina was someone I fucked around with, and that was sating hunger, but the moment I was close to Stasya, there was a pulse in my veins that I couldn't mistake. A deep hum in my body. And if Bromiel was anything to judge by, she felt it too.

To her credit, Stasya didn't flinch, only nodded. "It is fair, and he is right. He wishes to protect the wolves . . . not obliterate them." She turned to me, still a spark of mistrust and perhaps loathing in her gaze as she regarded me. "I promise myself to you."

"This is all my fault," Ansgar mumbled.

I turned to face him. "Sure as hell is. Now go out

there and tell them it's safe." Moving toward the side, I waited for him to announce to the guards that the coast was clear.

When he was far enough outside of the room, I slammed the door shut and twisted the lock. At once, the guards were in an uproar, but I had no intention of lingering.

Stasya bit her bottom lip and fiddled with a strand of her hair. It was uncharacteristic of her—at least from what I had seen. "What are you?"

"Aside from a wolf?" I asked quietly, moving the bottom of the mask down around my neck as I crept closer to her. "What do you think I am?"

"I don't know anything about our kind—but I feel . . ."

When I was mere inches from her, I used my finger to tilt her head back and stared into her bright green eyes. "What do you feel, princess?"

Stasya's cheeks reddened, and I opened my mouth to say something else, but then her mouth was on mine. My brows furrowed in question, but as she grew more confident in the kiss, I returned it. Her lips were soft against mine and spread heat throughout my body.

The noises she made only encouraged me to deepen the kiss, my fingers spreading across her back so I could tug her closer.

She plunged her tongue into my mouth, caressing mine, and I wanted nothing more than to hoist her onto my hips and lay her out on her father's bed.

In that moment, I felt it. We both did. We felt the call

and the desire of a bond that would last a lifetime. But this was not the moment to discuss it. Pulling back, I lifted the mask into place, winking at her. "I'll take what payment I can get for now. Stasya, stay inside, and do not venture out—none of the royal family. Trust only your kin. I will contact you soon."

"Niklaus!" She touched her lips, reaching for me as I backed away from her to the window.

I swung out of the bedroom window and climbed down the vines before I became one with the shadows.

Who's afraid of the Big Bad Wolf?

The Hawk definitely would be.

No need to wait. Jump back into the story with Stasya in Royal's Vow!

Stasya needs to rely on her instincts to discern friend from foe, or succumb to the perils that threaten to consume her kingdom and her very existence.

books2read.com/royalsvow

Acknowledgments

Thank you, dear reader, for taking the time to read Nik's story. He's been with me for a very long time! I hope you gained some insight as to how the Big Bad Wolf got his name and how the storybooks didn't get it quite right.

Originally, this was published as a Young Adult title, but it was never my intention to write Nik as a teen. In fact, he was meant to be 22-24 during the series, but due to needing to fit into a collection of other YA stories I had to age him down, which meant his story had to change a little, too.

Between a plethora of things such as a maximum word count, age limit, and content issues, it was admittedly rushed and not as fleshed out as I'd like. When I launched Midnight Tide Publishing I knew it was time to age Niklaus up! Buuuut… lots of other projects got in the way. So, here it is…FINALLY.

Yentl, this one is still for you!

A HUGE thank you to Tiss and Lou, you've been with Nik since the very beginning and I can't thank you enough for inspiring me in every way possible. Honestly, my two rocks in this writing industry.

Meg, my favorite comma goblin, thanks for always being there to pretty my babies up. You're my favorite comma goblin. <3

Special shoutout to Carla, Tiss, and Lou for constantly inspiring me to write new stories.

To my MTP crew, you have no idea how much all of you inspire me, and push me to be more creative, daring and prolific. Keep on writing, fam.

Donna, thank you for being a great Patreon! You've known Nik since he took his first breaths on a page, and I can't thank you enough for all of your support.

The Official Playlist

Want to listen along while you read and immerse yourself into the world of Hunter's Truce? Listen to the playlist below!

1. Dangerous by Royal Deluxe
2. New Blood Zade Wolf
3. Howling by Wild Rivers
4. Secret by Angel Snow
5. Run by AWOLNATION
6. Slow Dance With The Devil by Parson James
7. Born For This by Royal Deluxe
8. Won't Go Down Easy by Jaxson Gamble
9. Twisted by MISSIO
10. I'm A Wanted Man by Royal Deluxe

About Elle Beaumont

Elle Beaumont loves creating vivid and fantastical worlds. She lives in Southeastern Massachusetts with her husband and two children. When not writing or chasing around her children, she enjoys making candles. More than once she has proclaimed that coffee is the lifeblood and it is how she refrains from becoming a zombie.

Stay up to date and receive some free books by signing up for her newsletter! ellebeaumontbooks.com/newsletter

Join Elle's Facebook group and hang out with her facebook.com/groups/ElleBeaumontStreetTeam

For more information visit
www.ellebeaumontbooks.com
Follow Elle on social media!

facebook.com/ellebeaumontbooks
instagram.com/ellebeaumontbooks

MORE BOOKS YOU'LL LOVE

If you enjoyed this story, please consider leaving a review!

Then check out more books from Midnight Tide Publishing!

Of Flames & Curses by Whitney L. Spradling

Do fairies exist?

This is the question Lainey asks herself after her sister's brutal murder in Central Park. Armed with her sister's diary and the mysterious entries within, Lainey's quest for answers leads her to Phoenix, a surly but handsome fae.

The answer to Lainey's question reveals a truth that will change everything she thought she knew about herself and the world she lives in. A sacrifice must be made to break a curse that locked the gate between the human and faerie realms.

Leaving the only world she has known, Lainey finds herself surrounded by evil queens, curses, and magical creatures. Together, Lainey and Phoenix must find a way to break the curse that doesn't result in Lainey's death—like her sister's.

Available Now

The Songs That Beckon by M.A. Brown

Their grief binds them
The Song calls them
The Darkness wants to claim them

As winter wraps Areth in its frozen embrace, nightmarish beasts descend upon the Hastings household kidnapping Mr. and Mrs. Hastings and leaving behind their daughter, Bianca, as sole witness. In the wake of their abduction her quiet world is turned upside down and shaken revealing the secrets and lies her parents have buried.

As truths unravel it binds her to those who have similarly lost. Together they must wade through the thorny tangles of growing love and grief to find those that they hold dear before the looming threat of darkness is unleashed to destroy them all.

Available Now

9 781964 655031